Journey into the
Unknown

Journey into the unknown

Noorjehan

&

Adam Mahomed

EMBASSY BOOKS
www.embassybooks.in

First Published in India 2012

Published in India by :
Embassy Book Distributors
120 Great Western Building,
MCC Lane,
Kala Ghoda,
Fort,
Mumbai - 400023
India

Tel : +91-22-22819546 / 32967415
Email : info@embassybooks.in
Website : www.embassybooks.in

ISBN : 978-93-81860-39-7

In memory of my loving wife

Noorjehan

and my beautiful children

Shamima

Humeira

Nadia

Acknowledgements

How does one begin to say "thank you"?

I owe a vast debt to more people than I can mention.

I have to start with my family: my parents; my brothers – Aboo, Aziz, Sattar, Joe and Ali; my sisters Halima, Jeiboon and Jubeida; to all of you, a huge thank you for your unconditional and ongoing support, especially in the early days when we were most vulnerable to all sorts of delusions and figments of our imaginations.

Both Noorjehan, during her time, and I have fond memories of our superbly outstanding neighbours: Danny Gandhi (who sadly is no longer on the earthly plane) and his dear wife Fazila; Linda and Dee Pillay; Zarina and Ebrahim Moola; Julie and Whitey Jadwat; Sara and Harry Ramdhani. They were all a great source of inspiration and strength. Vasie and the late Hoosein were the anchor in our lives and literally took us by the hand and walked with us on that challenging road. Without their help our search for meaning would have been abandoned.

Thank you also to my nephews: Zuneit and Faiza; Haroon Gani; Solly Janoo, Farook Janoo; and Shiraz Gaffer, Ibrahim Ismail, together with my brother-in-law, Solly Latib.

To my long-time and cherished friends, Azra and Syed Choonara, Mario Rodriguez – you have been a pillar of strength.

Farida and Ahmed Randeree, who gave me invaluable assistance and encouragement when I was in the UK – I will always be beholden to you.

Our lawyer in the UK, Chris Wilson, for going beyond the call of duty and arranging a meeting with Doris Stokes. To Nine Merrington, thank you for your caring and support, may God bless you.

Anjana and Aziz Pahad, Meg and Essop Pahad, who have always been there for me – I am most grateful and moved by your ongoing support.

My amazing and caring staff: Ruth, Joyce, Karina, Romila, Melanie and Rejoice – you managed and maintained my surgery, giving me the space to cope with my grief. You have no idea how important it was for me at the time. Bless you!

The late Professor Fatima Meer, who encouraged Noorjehan to write and instilled in her the zeal and the mission to put pen to paper. May your soul rest in peace.

Zohra and Solly Noor: my heartfelt appreciation for your precious friendship.

After the demise of my beloved wife, my very dear friends, Saras and Saantha Naidu literally enveloped me in their arms, making it possible for me to handle my pain. Together with Paren Naidoo, Zee and Ahmed Suliman and Vinay Rajkumar they rallied to my side.

The absolute acme of comfort, caring and motivation is Jabu, Noorjehan's closest confidante and our housekeeper, who cried with me and simultaneously cared for me throughout my sad times. May God bless you, Jabu.

Ayesha Laher, whose visit to South Africa was very timely. You assisted me with all the rituals and formalities. You are a rare soul and your reward will be in heaven.

I am grateful to Aziz Hassim, who read the manuscript and made helpful constructive comments and suggestions. Thank you for stepping in at the last minute.

I am where I am through the love, prayers and encouragement of each of you. I honour and celebrate our friendship. May God in His grace reward all of you.

Prologue

After the brutal loss of our children, Noorjehan and I spent many an evening on our patio, talking softly, each counseling the other and making life somewhat bearable.

With the passage of time, the pain receded somewhat. We were able to converse a little rationally. That was when Noorjehan suggested that each of us should reduce our thoughts to writing.

It was a form of catharsis, a coping mechanism.

I welcomed the idea. We passed many an evening, silently recording our emotions. In its own way, it served to lessen the grief.

When Noorjehan passed away, this pursuit, like a house of cards, came to an abrupt end. Needless to say, I was totally devastated, shattered by her untimely departure.

Our writings ended up on a shelf in my study, gathering dust.

Somewhere along the way, the sight of these papers and the painful memories that they evoked, became too much to endure.

I decided that if I didn't do **something** with them they would affect my sanity.

However, I couldn't for a moment contemplate destroying them – I would effectively be destroying a vital link with my dear wife.

That was when a very special friend, to whom I shall be eternally indebted, suggested that I complete my part of the story and then publish the completed work. It would provide me with a degree of closure.

The more I thought about it, the more I liked the idea. What finally clinched the matter was when I reached the conclusion that the published document would serve, in some way, as a tribute to Noorjehan and a silent salutation to our love.

What you have in your hand now is a culmination of that decision.

Only time will tell whether it will, indeed, provide the closure I so desperately seek. But I do know this, with a certainty that cannot be denied, that Noorjehan is leaning over my shoulder, smiling and thanking me for this bouquet that I hold out to her.

May all gods be gentle to her soul.

– Adam

Foreword

It was our twenty-sixth wedding anniversary yesterday. We celebrated it quietly but happily with a few friends in our home. Adam had suggested going out for dinner, "I don't want you to be burdened with the cooking," he had said. It was no burden. I liked cooking and on those rare days when the veil of my grief lifted, I liked entertaining, dressing up my table and adorning it with the china and silver and the crystal that otherwise remain locked in the display cabinet.

It was one of those days. I would be a quiet hostess; Adam a spirited host. His laughter bubbling over the steam of akhni. I would imagine a young lady standing next to me, my eldest daughter, twenty-four years old, as pretty as a picture, asking me if she should bring more *akhni*. "Shamima, my darling," I would say, my voice low under my breath but Adam would hear, and he quickly would draw me out of my momentary trance and at the same time distract our guests. I heard him say, "Noorjehan makes the best akhni in town, but today she has exceeded herself," and he would reassuringly squeeze my hand. The guests would remain oblivious to the fleeting drama at the head of the table. I would thank Allah for the vision he had granted me of our eldest daughter, as she would have been had she lived: tall, beautiful, my pillar of strength. I later told Adam about my vision and he would confirm the reality of it. He would say he had never seen such brightness in my eyes as at that moment when I had seemed lost to him and to our guests.

Such fleeting visions, or should I say visitations, have come to me on several occasions and they have comforted me in my grief. It is a grief I share with my husband, an excruciating, inconsolable grief as sharp today as it was when it suddenly came upon us with the deaths of our three daughters, Shamima, Nadia and Humeira, in one fatal accident.

– Noorjehan

EVEN THIS WILL PASS AWAY

Once in Persia reigned a king,
Who upon a signet ring
Carved a maxim strange and wise,
When held before his eyes,
Gave him counsel at a glance,
Fit for every change and chance:
Solemn words and these they were:
"EVEN THIS WILL PASS AWAY"

Trains of camel through the sand
Brought him gems from Samarcand;
Fleets of galleys over the seas
Brought him pearls to rival these,
But he counted little gain,
Treasures of the mine or main:
"What is wealth?" the king would say,
"EVEN THIS WILL PASS AWAY"

Mid the pleasures of his court
At the zenith of their sport,
When the palms of all his guests
Burned with clapping at his jests,
Seated midst the figs and wine,
Said the king: "Ah, friends of mine,
Pleasure comes but not to stay,"
"EVEN THIS WILL PASS AWAY"

Woman, fairest ever seen
Was the bride he crowned as queen,
Pillowed on the marriage-bed
Whispering to his soul, he said
"Though no monarch ever pressed
Fairer bosom to his breast,

Mortal flesh is only clay!
"EVEN THIS WILL PASS AWAY"

Fighting on the furious field,
Once a javelin pierced his shield,
Soldiers with a loud lament
Bore him bleeding to his tortured side,
"Pain is hard to bear," he cried
"But with patience, day by day,
"EVEN THIS WILL PASS AWAY"

Towering in a public square
Forty cubits in the air,
And the king disguised, unknown,
Gazed upon his sculptured name,
And he pondered, "What is fame?
Fame is but a slow decay!
"EVEN THIS WILL PASS AWAY"

Struck with palsey, sore and old,
Waiting at the gates of gold,
Said he with his dying breath
"Life is done, but what is Death?"
Then an answer to the king
Fell a sunbeam on his ring;
Showing by a heavenly ray,
"EVEN THIS WILL PASS AWAY"

– THEODORE TILTEN

One

NOORJEHAN: I was raised in a typical Muslim shop-keeping family in the then Transvaal in South Africa (the area now known as Gauteng). My father was a shopkeeper. My father and his three brothers had grown up in my grandfather's shop as had my two sisters, my brother and I. My grandfather's shop was the original family business. From this, other businesses developed.

My father, for reasons I never knew, was treated like the black sheep of the family and this had a bad effect on him. It undermined his self-confidence. This is how my mother saw it and this is how we understood it through her. My mother was not one to accept being married to a black sheep. She rebelled against it. She challenged my father; she challenged his family. They resented this. It was not her place as a daughter-in-law to disrupt the family peace, and as far as they were concerned, she had no right to re-arrange my father's position in the family. They hated her for it, and she hated them back with all the venom she could muster in her breast. All this hating took its toll upon her. It left her an embittered, damaged woman, so much so, that when it came to us, her daughters, she could not give us the little love and support we needed. The little tenderness that she still possessed she gave to her son. So when I was stricken with my terrible grief there was little she could or would do for me, apart from turning her eyes heavenwards and saying, "It is in Allah's hands."

My mother's rebellion in her mother-in-law's house had a positive result; it jerked my father out of his resignation to his black sheep position; and my mother's passion to be liberated from her mother-in-law's house eventually changed him. He left his parental home and business and set out on his own. My mother provided the initial capital, the meagre sum of fifty rands that she had saved.

It was a brave plunge and it paid off. We were proud as a family when my father opened our shop, "The Middleburg Cash Store".

We started with a comparatively tiny stock, but the empty boxes lining our shelves gave the impression of a wealth of goods. I still remember our first sale – it was a ballpoint pen for fifteen cents.

For shop assistants were my father's daughters. We didn't all start together. My eldest sister, Ruby was the first to join him and she served him the longest. Sheila was the second – when she married and moved to Durban, Ruby was forced to leave school and serve in the shop. I left school when Ruby married and worked there until my own marriage. By then my father's business had prospered and he had the means to employ shop assistants.

We girls were good at our jobs and we provided a good service under our father's direction. The empty boxes were soon replaced with genuine ones, filled with real stock as the wholesale firms gained confidence in us and began supplying us with goods on credit. Our success was threatened by the hostility of other shopkeepers, who intimidated and pressurised the wholesalers if they supplied us with goods. My father very wisely responded by concentrating on women's wear that the others did not stock.

We had everything a woman required – curtaining, dress fabric, haberdashery, underwear, ready-to-wear garments, baby clothes, school uniforms, ladies' hats, you name it. If we did not have an item we ordered it. My father's philosophy was based on a small profit and a large turnover; never allow a customer to leave without buying something. We were all schooled in this and woe betide any of us who did not make a sale. If a customer came in for an item and we did not have it, our instruction was to show her something close to it and make a sale. Hell broke loose if a customer left empty-handed.

Our clientele was mainly Afrikaners and we addressed them as "Mevrou" and "Meneer" and at times "Missus" and "Baas".

There was a time when our business hit a rough patch. It eventually recovered but we had to scrimp and save in the first few years. My mother took in sewing to make ends meet; our curries were diluted with water, our food purchases were in pennies and tickeys. I recall going to the Greek shop to purchase a tickey's worth of tomatoes. A tickey was all my mother could

15

spare. The greengrocer obliged the first few times but then it got too much for him and he booted me out of his shop with, "I got nothing for a tickey, you come with a sixpence, you hear, if you want any tomatoes at all!"

On occasion we ate sumptuously on Eid: biryani and samoosas and we dressed prettily. We spent the night before uncomfortably in dinky curlers, and mehndi-spread palms wrapped up in bandages, but on the day of Eid, we were like fairies in our curls and our new dresses. It was an occasion for a photograph and we went to the white photographer who posed us before his camera and recorded our prettiness for posterity.

Our house was small and frugally furnished. There were two bedrooms; my parents occupied the one, and we three sisters the other. My brother slept in the dining room. We had a red and grey lounge suite which was my mother's pride and joy. She had it covered in plastic to protect it. I hated those plastic covers. You slipped and slid on them and if you sat too long you got stuck to them. We had no wardrobes and our clothes were kept in boxes under the bed.

A great change came into our lives when my father installed a shower in the bathroom. It was a sign of our growing prosperity. Another sign was the grey and pink panelite kitchen suite my father bought. It raised a furore in the family because one of my father's brothers or his wife objected to my mother having something they didn't have. My mother, proud and defiant, insisted my father return it, my father insisted it stay. I returned from school each afternoon expecting it to be gone and was relieved each afternoon to find it still there. I loved that panelite suite. It stayed.

Our parents could not afford to keep all of us in school. The girls were the first to be forced to discontinue their education. My eldest sister Ruby, was the one who gave the most of herself to the family. She was expected to make all the sacrifices and she made them dutifully and, apparently, happily. She interrupted her schooling in Pretoria and came to help my father in the business. My second sister, Sheila, was allowed to complete her junior certificate examination; only my brother was left to continue his schooling. Sheila spent very little time in the shop. Prettier than Ruby, she caught the fancy of a young man from a very wealthy family in Durban and was in a whirlwind romance before I could get to spend any time with her. I had the impression that she was too absorbed in herself to even know of my existence. Neither did she show any sympathy for Ruby, who became the butt of our pity for being "left on the shelf" while the youngest sister was betrothed. Ruby ignored the clucking taunts and was happy for Sheila. I was the youngest child. I had to fend for myself at an early age. I received very little formal education.

Sheila was the first to marry. Her wedding was a grand affair and she made a fabulous bride. My parents were relieved that one of their three daughters was suitably married but worried about Ruby's "spinstership" at twenty-something. But their worry was short-lived. My maternal uncle's son, pious and caring by nature, mercifully ended that state and rescued her from the taunts and sympathies she suffered. The family was nowhere as wealthy as Sheila's husband's, but it was a good family and Ruby was duly married.

I missed Ruby when she left us. It seemed to me that she had been the only one who tolerated my growing years; but on the whole, I grew up all by myself; in my father's shop, in my mother's house, at school in Middleburg, among my friends, my sisters, my brother and my stray cats.

I loved those cats. I seduced them with bowls of milk slipped out of the kitchen when my mother was not looking. The cats became my friends and there was no one but them who used to await my return from school. My friendship with the cats ended abruptly when one of them gave birth to her kittens on my bed whilst I was asleep. My mother was aghast and very angry at being left with the cleaning. "No more cats in the house!" she ordered, and as much as I pined for them, I had no option but to abide by her rules.

I had a special friend at school, Shaida, who was deaf and dumb but as bright as a new sixpence. With specialised tutoring, she could have gone far, but this was not available in Middleburg, so she sat with us in the normal class and I came to understand her and interpreted for her to others. Shaida trusted me and emulated me and this made me feel proud and responsible. There was a day when some inspectors came from Cape Town and they spoke to me and then to Shaida sitting next to me. I interpreted for her and they were very impressed. They went to my father at the shop and tried to persuade him to allow me to accompany Shaida to a special school in Cape Town. My father was too busy with his customers to pay much attention. He tossed away their suggestions as absurd and totally untenable. Shaida's parents were no more receptive than mine. Her fate was sealed to be a deaf mute all her life and serve her family and help her mother with her home industry. Shaida was very good wth her hands, with needlework and embroidery, cooking and housework. But I knew that she was very intelligent and would have gone far if she had just had the opportunity. Instead, my dear friend was relegated to a life of drudgery.

In my child's world, I was beginning to think that grown-ups didn't do the right thing by their children. I felt shut-off by them. It was a matter of "Speak when spoken to!" and "Keep your opinions to yourself". In fact, I was not supposed to have any opinions.

My sister Ruby, was my refuge. She talked to me, she counselled me, but the couselling came from her own bleak experience and it was to restrain me, to warn me to expect no more of life than what was under my nose – the shop, the house with its frugal furniture and parents who instructed us but showed little affection outwardly, and if there was some inwardly, we never came to know of it.

I was the last of my parents' three daughters to be married. My parents began thinking of settling me down the moment I turned into a leggy teenager. When I turned sixteen I was introduced, perhaps I should say presented, to a young man. A suitable life partner for me, my mother said. He was a doctor, and my family felt he would give me security and status, but after a few meetings with him I realised that we were totally incompatible. The arrangements had been made entirely between our respective parents. My friends teased me about him and his friends teased him about me, but that was as far as the romance went. The engagement didn't last. I don't recall the exact circumstances leading to the breakdown but something quite irreconcilable happened between our parents.

It was not acceptable in our community for a girl to have her engagement broken. It left her with a stigma. My mother was very worried lest I end up on the shelf. So she rushed me into accepting the second proposal. While I was disinterested in the first young man, I positively disliked the second. But I could not shake off the pressure from my parents and sisters. I was eighteen, they pointed out, a ripe old age. Most girls were mothers by that age and here was I, single. I could end up a spinster, they said. And to my disadvantage was the fact that I already had one broken engagement behind me. Under the circumstances, I was told that I was lucky that I had received this proposal at all.

I finally buckled under their pressure. The serbert was drunk and mouths sweetened with all sorts of cardamom flavoured sweetmeats, made in pure ghee and the creamiest of milk. Gifts were exchanged and gold jewellery showered upon me. The young man was keenly interested in me, but I discovered that his mother wasn't. She totally disapproved of me. She thought me too modern. I would have to live in this family, headed by his mother. I realised it would be an impossible situation. Not having the guts to face him, I wrote him a letter breaking off the engagement. He was very upset and sent his elders to persuade me to reconsider. His mother was a widow and needed her son. I decided not to come between them. My family was devastated. I had now broken two engagements! My father tried to reason with me. It was a good match, he came from a good family, he was diligent and conscientious. What more did I want? At that point in my life, I didn't know what I wanted. Perhaps just to be left alone with my shopkeeping and cycling and giggling with my girlfriends. When that engagement broke, my parents' displeasure knew no bounds. I think it was only my usefulness as a shop assistant that prevented them from washing their hands of me entirely.

Two

ADAM: I am Adam Mahomed. I was born in 1940, in a small Afrikaner dorp in the then Transvaal. It's a little town called Balfour. It lies between Heidelberg and Standerton. The time of my birth was not auspicious – the Second World War was raging. I doubt that my parents welcomed me as a gift from God, as is customary. But, innocent of the tribulations of the time, my brothers and sisters would have received me with great excitement as is the nature of young children on seeing a new baby.

I come from a fairly large family. We were eight brothers and three sisters.

My father had a general dealers' shop, as had his brothers. They sold everything, from a pin to an elephant, as it is proverbially said. The shops had store rooms and these provided the children with private play space, encouraging secrets and the pursuit of activities that the elders frowned upon.

An incident I remember vividly is when a friend and I were playing in a storeroom and a bee stung him and, of course, there was immediate swelling. As we ran from the yard and into the street, passing all the shops, with my friend screaming and crying and obviously in pain (the shops were in a row) everyone stopped to ask him what had happened. He then decided to complain that a bee had stung him. I couldn't understand why the same question was being asked repeatedly, more so when he was screaming the answer to all and sundry. What confused me even more was why he didn't simply run home and have his affliction attended to. Why stop everywhere? I could only assume that he was reveling in all the sympathy that he was receiving.

Another time that I remember quite well was when we must have been about 5 or 6 years old. In those days there were no primary or pre-nursery schools. As a result, it was interesting listening to all the school boys talking about how they jumped classes and I suppose due to age, if they had been older, they'd have been put into a higher class.

Those were very good times. We played a lot of outdoor games. One of the games was with three tins and we used sticks. One big stick, one long stick, and a short stick, which was very popular.

We were also crazy about soccer and cricket. Soccer was really amazing and we used to love playing soccer and cricket on the school grounds. It was a good time in our lives. I suppose the past always seems to be good to us. We always believe that however bad the past may have been, it was the best time of our lives.

I remember sometime in 1946-47, I was then about 7 years old, when my father had bought an old Buick. Obviously, in those days, we had but one car for the whole family – although we were eleven in the family and some of my brothers were married – and we all piled in with gusto, each commandeering a place of his own.

When I was about seven years old, I joined my brothers at a school in Standerton (which is 50 miles away from Balfour). Initially we stayed at a hostel, but it meant having to live away from home. Feeling alone, I did a little crying but did not want to seem like a sissy. So, I used to cry in my own time and in my own way, and in the privacy of my room. I needed to feel that I was a man and could stay away from home. I suppose we were socialised at a very tender age to accept the dynamics that boys don't cry and only girls have that privilege.

I was also secure in the knowledge that I had two brothers at the school who were older than me. Knowing that, it comforted me. And I enjoyed school. I loved playing marbles and obtained immense pleasure from the occasional game of soccer.

These were all learning years for us, and it was a beautiful time.

We stayed in the hostel which adjoined our school in Standerton, a small town. The hostel was run by a Muslim lady and its nearness to all the amenities made it very easy for us to get around.

The headmaster's name was a Mr Le Roux and he was quite strict. He was not averse to using the cane – not too hard but hard enough to still feel it the next day. Most of the time I was punished for getting to school late in the morning. This was my brother's fault, as he was seldom ready on time. I threatened to go ahead on my own and made it clear that if anything untoward happened to me, my parents would hold him responsible. That sorted the problem out, quite satisfactorily though not entirely.

At midday on each Friday, we had to make our obeisance to God, the Creator. We had to ensure that we were spotlessly clean before entering the mosque and this presented us with a massive problem. All we had was a bucket of water, not particularly hot, and it had to serve many of us at the same time. Somehow, we managed. And prayed fervently that God would reward us for our efforts.

As some wit once said: they were the best of times, they were the worst of times.

I must admit, though, that we loved going to school. We had a huge playground and they gave us little pieces of cheese. Wow!! That was great! Even though we now have the choice of all the best cheeses in the world, where I am right now, that taste was better than any of the other cheeses I have ever eaten, possibly because we were given small portions at the school.

The bane of our life was attending the madressa – the Islamic school. With one solitary exception, the other teachers swore by the adage: punishment, punishment and more punishment. And for the most trivial infringement. All it achieved was a hatred for the place and a greater hatred for our tutors.

As an institution of learning, it failed miserably. We were taught to read the Quran, in Arabic. We didn't understand a word of it, and that was not entirely as a result of it not being in our language of communication – the reality was that our teachers were from India, and they themselves **did not understand Arabic**.

The entire exercise was done in parrot fashion – by both the tutors (so-called) and the students. And, because they were paid very poorly, the teachers' frustrations were visited on the learners.

I remember when we used to go to Balfour by train, which took about two hours from Standerton. It was quite easy getting to the railway station and the train stopped almost opposite our shop, so that was quite nice – the train rides. Every holiday we would go home and then, when we returned to school, our parents used to drop us off because we used to bring lots of other stuff like biscuits and cheeses, etc. to enjoy back at the hostel.

I remember another time, in 1948, when my second brother got married. That was in Standerton and at that time I had to have all my hair removed – it is a sort of traditional thing – and obviously it was terrible, but I had a cap on and it looked very nice. And now we had an extra home to go to because my brother had his own house.

Going to the cinema on a Saturday afternoon was a dangerous pastime – the little white hooligans would lie in wait for us and viciously attack us without us provoking them in any way.

At times, it was okay, on other times it was bad. And, although we knew that if we ganged up we could have beaten them up, can you imagine doing that in the apartheid days? If you dared to defend yourself they would come over and beat you up right in your school. And, of course, the law was on their side. So, we always played a cat and mouse game with them. This, somehow, when I look back, hardened us. It prepared us for life. We realised, even at such a young age, that growing up in that apartheid society required us to always be vigilant and prepared for anything. It was a rule – the first rule of survival.

The cinema in Standerton was for whites only – strange but true. There were a few seats reserved for non-whites. They had given us the seats right at the back, on the upper floor, because they said that all the "Coolies" should only be sitting up there. The seats were hard, yes, but it was good because one would have thought that they would like to take the upper floor, you know, upstairs, but I suppose they wanted to see the cinema, the film, before us.

I remember we looked forward to seeing Tarzan and the Apes. That was our favourite. It was like the whole week you'd be anticipating what the next chapter would bring. Would Tarzan win or could the Apes win? So it was in suspense that the week passed. Of course, that was in serial form. And then, obviously, that was followed by the film. They refer to them as soapies now.

And then there was Movietone – about the world news. It was very informative. We followed the war. We lived in our little worlds. And we dreamed our dreams!

In those days we got sixpence a day allowance – and that was a lot of spending money. The three of us brothers, Aziz, Satar and I, each got sixpence a day. There was a shop known as Kajee's that sold chips and they were soaked in spices, the masala chips – together with red chillies and vinegar. It cost us a tickey each, so Aziz and myself normally bought those chips.

My late brother Satar, loved his chocolate ice cream, which cost sixpence. The ice creams being so little, he'd finish it fairly quickly and then he would take our two tickey's away, to make another sixpence for another ice cream. We always gave it to him willingly because we were quite full with the chips anyway. Somehow those chips tasted quite unique in the sense that you had so little, so that sixpence was so precious to us. It was like we had a lot of money.

We always bitched around our parents about how bad the hostel was, because everybody wanted to go back home. In reality, the food wasn't too bad and the old lady was pretty good. But some of us were from Delmas, some from Balfour, and others from Heidelberg, and we just wanted to get back home. Naturally, we preferred the food at home rather than the food at Standerton. So bitching became standard practice.

I stayed on for two years at Standerton. During the course of that time my brother Satar, was a problem to my dad, because every time they brought him back to school he would hold on to the tyres and refuse to come to Standerton. I feel sure it broke my father's heart, as Satar would just cry and scream, and cry and scream, and would not get into the car. I did not feel that bad for him at the time because I thought he's older than me and he needs to come to school.

That was when my father decided that there was a crying need for a school in Balfour – perhaps providing tuition up to the sixth grade only, for starters. There was a reasonably large Indian population to ensure a full student body. And my father, together with some of the other Indian families, was prepared to contribute to its costs. He instructed my eldest brother, Kareem, to approach the Ministry of Education. As a result, two years later, in 1949, we had our school.

So, we had a school in Balfour. It was a very small school, not as big as the one in Standerton and obviously, we were fairly old by then – we didn't start school at age six but we started it at seven. It was a rule at the time, an unwritten rule, that your age determined the standard you were in. As a result, many of us simply jumped a standard or two.

For a change, the student population now came into Balfour, and the number of students from nearby towns increased. For us, school became a pleasure now, because it was just up the road and we could enjoy home cooked meals every day.

We had good facilities there. We had excellent soccer grounds, beautiful cricket fields, though not all on the school ground, as it was a little distance away. They belonged to the Indian soccer club and the Indian cricket club. They were pretty small but they loved their sport – there was not much else to do in those days.

Our principal was a Mr Kather. He was very good for the school because he was from Durban, which was famous for its high education standard, and he had the tenacity to make this an outstanding school, which he gradually did. He was strict. He was a disciplinarian, but he was gentle. He was a good man on the whole. He was huge in size but he was soft and gentle and he took a personal interest in all his students.

At the time, for my father, life was good. He had managed to get a school opened in Balfour, his business was thriving and his sons were doing well. And then, in 1952, tragedy struck. We attended the wedding of a cousin – my brother's best friend – it was on the farm, Grootvlei, where the mines are. In those days all the roads were gravel roads.

Three

ADAM: The first tragedy we suffered as a family was the death of my brother on the gravel road while driving in a friend's bakkie. My brother was hurt and unconscious. The occupants in the opposite car, which consisted of a white couple, were okay, they were not badly hurt. The two Indian guys were pretty badly hurt, because my brother's friend Essa, had broken his legs, and my brother was unconscious. When the ambulance from Balfour arrived, it took the white occupants of the car which had smashed into my brother's vehicle and refused to take the Indian casualties. As they said, "You're Indian and you're not allowed into this white ambulance." It took another hour and a half for an ambulance to come from Heidelberg because they had non-white services there. This ambulance took the injured to the general hospital in Johannesburg. I now realise that, but for Apartheid and the colour bar, my brother's life would have been saved.

We made daily visits to Johannesburg to see my brother. We were kids and we didn't know how severe and how serious his condition was. I often asked my elder brother what was going to happen and he said, "Well, you know, he may lose his eye," but I thought, well that's okay really; that he was in a coma did not worry me. Losing an eye is not that bad. My father and mother stayed over in Johannesburg and my grandfather from Pretoria came every day.

My brother had two children then and they were quite young, just seven and five. One is now a doctor and the other is a businessman. My brother died seven days later and I remember the preacher telling us that he would go to heaven and this was the only thing we talked about the next day at school. All we talked about was how he would be going to heaven and what heaven would be like, and we did not realise how much we were crying.

Before that, my father used to play cards with his friends. He gave up on that, and suddenly he changed. He was good to his children but he was not jovial, not as jovial as he used to be. Now, I understand why.

I was 12 years old at the time, and deeply pained by the incident, although I'm sure not as much as it affected my parents.

Sometimes we think that, at the age of seven, the whole world lives for us. The trees and the sun come out for us, the flowers bloom for us, and our parents treat us like little emperors. Unfortunately, like all good things, this comes to an end.

It has been said that every seven years our body undergoes a change. This means that in the space of 70 years your body has changed, all your cells, your mind, your thinking have all changed ten times. So, up to the age of seven, they refer to it as a masturbatory stage. You are self satisfied. And suddenly you are 12 years old and you see the tragedy of your life.

And then you are 14 years old! At that stage, we pretend that we do not like girls very much. Of course, we did like the girls but we wouldn't show it because we'd be called sissies. And so, right up to the ages of 12, 13, 14, I think these friendships we developed were just the best types of friendship we could have at that stage, and that they would supposedly last your lifetime.

And at that stage we did not socialise much, we did not run around with girls, the boys were boys and the girls were girls. We were most probably in what we could call the male bonding stage.

We may not have realised it, but because we had to go to Standerton to school, away from our home town, we were much more exposed than a lot of people would have been. We were very young, we were impressionable and we were sort of independent at that stage because we had to care for ourselves. We didn't have our mums to cuddle us, we didn't have our dads there, we were at a hostel, the people at the hostel had obviously their own problems, so they had no time to mother and father us.

With the establishment of the school in Balfour, all that changed. We were happier there. We played soccer at our local club with an African team from the location and the whites were disgusted and said, "How can you play soccer with Africans?"

forgetting that we were also treated as second class citizens.

It is very difficult to understand why they would object, because we were totally marginalised. We were not white enough. We were a type of refuse to the Nationalist Party and, if they could have, they would have got rid of us.

Anyway, I completed my schooling in Balfour, where I did my Standard Six and the following year, because we did not have a non-white high school in Balfour, my uncle phoned my dad and told him that in Rustenburg they had just started a high school and they had to have a certain amount of pupils to be granted the status of being a secondary school.

My father decided that I needed to go to Rustenburg. My mother's sister lived there so I stayed with her to do my Standards Seven and Eight.

Four

ADAM: My uncle was very poor and he had four sons and three daughters. I stayed with them in their house, although he was working as a poorly paid rep for some company. My uncle, Ibrahim Abba, was a good man and my aunty was an amazing woman. In my time there, almost 18 to 20 months, I never heard her scream or raise her voice once. She was a very gentle woman, she was a very kind woman, she was quite a unique woman. My mother would scream and shout at times but I never heard her sister behave that way. She was just one of those women who was very patient with her life, with her children, with everything around her. As a result she was much liked in Rustenburg. She treated me as one of her own, and I could never forget her and I always had prayed for her. Although later in life she became bedridden, I somehow couldn't get myself to go and see her in that condition. I remembered the better days, I remembered the beautiful days. She was a very good looking woman and very saintly.

So I stayed in Rustenburg with them and I attended the Rustenburg High School. We had an Afrikaner principal, I think his name was Sitebottom. He always told us that when we spelt his name it should not be a double u but it should be a wobble-u sort of thing! I didn't, and none of the other students for that matter, understood what that was supposed to mean.

Some of our teachers were South Indian gentlemen from Durban. It was the time when they were trying to do away with white teachers in Indian schools. One of the Indian teachers, a Mr Naidoo from Durban, was very good. He taught us mathematics. I was there for two years and I finished off my Standard Eight. I still salute Mr Naidoo – a true educationist.

In 1955, my brother Karrim, was murdered. Murdered by my cousins. My father and his brother had a dispute over a property which we, the younger generation, weren't aware of. My father and my eldest brother were negotiating with my uncle to amicably resolve the matter.

One Sunday evening, we were outside the school in one of the cars: my two brothers, all their friends plus my cousin who later murdered my brother. There was a very attractive young lady at the teacher's house. We went there simply to ogle at this beauty, the teacher's sister. She was a very, very attractive woman.

It was while we were sitting in the car, it must have been around seven o'clock and my cousin – whom we subsequently came to discover – murdered my brother, came to ask where Karrim was. I replied that he probably would be doing some books at his office. I had no reason to suspect an ulterior motive.

The next day, when my brother did not pitch up at the shop, my father asked my brother Abu to go and check out where he was and when Abu went to Karrim's room he found that the bed had not been slept in. Abu then looked for him in the usual places but failed to find him. When Abu reported to my father his inability to locate Karrim, my dad was quite shocked. Karrim had never failed to inform my dad of his movements so my dad naturally suspected that something was very wrong.

At about eleven o'clock that morning, my father closed the shop and we were standing outside. My cousins had just come through with their Buick car. We asked them if they knew where Karrim was and they said, "No," they did not know as they had been to my uncle's place at the farm. My father became suspicious and he said, "How is that possible? I've phoned him and he said nobody was there." My father then phoned my other cousins and, when they too denied seeing Karrim, my father reported the matter to the police.

The police, in the course of their investigation, called at my uncle's place. As they went in they found my cousins cleaning the Buick because the car was full of blood, as were their offices and the area around it. The three brothers and the dad were arrested and charged with murder.

They were tried at the Supreme Court in Pretoria, and I was called to give evidence. I must have been about 16 or 17 years old at the time. I was kept in the witness box for an hour or an hour and a half. My cousins had engaged Issie Maisels, one of the top advocates in South Africa together with Vernon Berrange, also one of the country's top advocates. They had another distinguished legal man, Advocate De Wet. They kept trying to confuse me regarding the time factor. But when you're stating the truth, which we were doing, it's very difficult to create confusion. You have this certainty in your mind, and it's very difficult to shake that conviction.

I kept to my story and they couldn't shake me. All of them were found guilty and, for some inexplicable reason, the judge discharged all of them. We felt there was some element of bribery or corruption, but we were not quite certain, and could not prove it.

The prosecutor appealed and they were brought up on the lesser count of manslaughter. We had to go to court for a second time and once again I had to appear in court and give evidence. It taught me a lot about life. It was scary in the witness box, we were young and inexperienced and we did not have any idea how, during the cross-examination, they try to break you down.

My dad was totally devastated. I had to leave school and help with the business. As time went by, our business grew exponentially. We became quite big and became a major enterprise in the locality. My uncle and his family were not doing well, people were calling them "murderers" and they lost a lot of business.

Strange, how life unfolds. They hoped that by eliminating my brother, they would destroy our business. But life does not pan out as you always plan it. The saying that "Man proposes, God disposes", is so true because we make many plans about how we would like the future to be, but because life is so uncertain, life is a gamble and because life is a gamble there is much uncertainty.

Some people think that they are indispensible but life teaches us, over a period of time, that nobody is indispensible and life just carries on. My brother's murder brought that lesson home quite forcefully. I had some misgivings about the future of our business. Karrim had been a livewire and I doubted that we could carry on without him. Somehow, and strangely enough, our business grew from strength to strength.

When I joined the business I initially worked in the hardware department. Later, I moved into the clothing section and then managed the grocery store. When, a few years later, we opened a huge furniture business next door, I was exposed to a new world and a new business ethic.

A little later, we ventured into the world of motor cars. We regularly travelled to Johannesburg and Durban. In those days driving to Durban was a rare treat, and whenever we went there to buy and collect cars, we obtained much pleasure from the journey. Business really boomed when we started buying and selling tractors. For me, it was a tremendous learning curve.

You feel proud of your achievements. I don't think it was an ego thing. There was an element of pride, of a job well done and the warm glow of success and a sense of achievement. The business continued to grow and our life revolved around it. Our day normally began at eight o'clock and ended after six in the evening.

We had a huge dining table, around which we gathered for supper. My father, after having eaten, would go up to the main room in the house and leave us alone. He was aware that we were all smokers and he gave us our space. It was a simple matter of respect. Our lives regained a degree of normality after the tragedy of my brother's murder.

Weekends were brilliant, really, because on Sunday we used to play cards until late and open baked beans and sardines and they were good times.

Five

ADAM: I was about 22 and, having done matric privately, on a part time basis, I asked my dad whether it was possible for me to go to a trade school or something of that sort and he said, "Well, your cousin is in Karachi, Pakistan. Why don't you phone him?" I did exactly that and my cousin thought it was a huge joke, and he said, "Yeah, why don't you come over?" And so, the next day my father decided "Okay, you better go there." And I said, "Well, that's very quick!" and he said, "Look, if you're thinking of going, you had better go." Of course, I had cold feet and I thought to myself, "I haven't touched a book for years and what happens if I'm unsuccessful?" I really wouldn't want to come back as a failure as that would devastate my pride, my ego, everything.

That was when my brother had a great idea, "Tell everybody you're going on a business trip, so people will not have expectations of you."

And so, as I flew off to Karachi, I was thinking, "Wow, great, I'm going to travel abroad." But in those days there was a lot of poverty in India and Pakistan. But we had a 45th cutting – some connection from the village – and the first day I got to his place after I reached Karachi, I found that he had a son who was somewhat retarded. As a South African I was very fussy, especially about cleanliness and table manners. On my first day at a table with the son, I was quite thrown off balance. This fellow's hands were all over the plate and I refused to eat, but how long does one refuse to eat? Ultimately, I said, "Okay, it doesn't matter really. It's a bit messy but I need to fill myself up!"

These are lessons we learn in our lives and travel certainly broadens the horizon. But Pakistan was wonderful. It was an amazing experience. Yet I was homesick, I wanted to go back home. That, however, was out of the question. I had to stay and obtain a qualification of some sort.

They have a system there, where you do two years Inter-Science and then you can get admission to medical school. I was able to complete that requirement with comparative ease.

I did the first year and came home for a visit, and then went back to Karachi and completed the second year. These are important exams because they determine your future – whether you get into medical school or dental school or not. As I finished my exams I had a telegram from home saying that my mother had had a stroke.

I returned to South Africa. My mum was unconscious and our family was devastated so I stayed on for two months until I received the news that I had passed my exams and had done reasonably well. I decided that I needed to get back. My mother had partially recovered. She was conscious, but she was paralysed and in a wheelchair.

On my return to Pakistan, I joined the International Students' Organisation. This presented me with a problem: apart from sport, I knew little about South Africa's GDP, population numbers, inflation and growth prospects. So I had to do some extensive reading, to catch up pretty fast, to avoid appearing to be stupid when asked related questions by the other members.

During the course of my second year in Pakistan, the International Students' Organisation had an election and I was asked to attend. Somebody then decided that I should be nominated to the post of the secretary of this body. I immediately stood down, making it clear that I had little experience for such a job. However, my friend talked me into it and said that he had been secretary for quite a few associations and he would assist me in that function. I very relucantly took up the post, which was most challenging, obviously. I'd never prepared minutes in my life and knew little of meeting procedure and conduct. And as I took up the post, I thought it was a good thing that had happened to me.

This was another avenue that had opened and broadened the scope of my vision.

An item that stands out in my mind is when the International

Student's Organisation was invited by the Rotary Club to give a talk. We had about 15 representatives from countries, and the Rotary was keen to hear from all of them. The intention was to have one student representative from each country to give a talk on his or her country's contribution to World Peace and World Prosperity.

As the South African representative, we had chosen a lady by the name of Sara Jadwat, and we started doing some research, going to the library quite often just to learn what our country had contributed. Sadly, there wasn't anything significant that we could home in on. Of course, we had sent troops to fight in the Second World War, but that was not particularly meritorious, as almost all other countries being represented had done likewise.

And then we stumbled on a juicy topic: we had contributed to the elimination of locusts. So we prepared to talk on that. However, we were totally out of our depth. And, as a result, we did not have the confidence required to hold our own and, to make matters worse, our president decided to get ill and I had to lead the delegation. As I sat down I had the Ambassador of America on my right, one of the Pakistani Ministers on my left and, across from me, the English Ambassador. I was totally intimidated. I'd never been in such an august gathering!

During dinner, we were served soup for starters. As a country hick, from the backwood town of Balfour, I had no idea how to partake of it. And, being in the company of such distinguished pesonages, I was completely overawed. All I could do was imitate the others.

I managed to hold my own until, to my horror, a fly landed in my soup. Unsure of what to do next, I kept pushing the fly to the side of the bowl and making a show of sipping the soup, until a waiter appeared at my side and I quietly passed the bowl to him. When I subsequently asked my colleagues what I should have done they, laughingly, simply said that I should have called a waiter. Easily said, not so easily done – calling a waiter would have drawn attention to me, and that was the last thing I wanted.

With the meal out of the way I was just beginning to relax when, to my dismay, I was called to make my speech. It was my first speech, and my stomach was fluttering with butterflies.

Somehow, I managed to read my speech and felt very good after that. And, as I was congratulated by the ambassadors I thought, "Well, now I've graduated. You've gone from the atmosphere to the stratosphere!" And it was a time when I could validate myself. I could say, "Okay, now I've had the experience and I did not make a total fool of myself."

In retrospect, I often think, "Well, that was great really," I believed it could have been a big turning point in my life. I thought at that time, "Wow, I didn't even know, coming from South Africa had not taught us all that. I would not mind my children becoming ambassadors and ministers."

This thought was the result of experiencing a free world, a democratic society where we could socialise and associate as we chose – and it made us realise that we could achieve whatever we could conceive, without hindrance and restriction.

It was a liberating experience.

Six

ADAM: On completing my Inter-Science studies, I decided to pursue that avenue a little further. I found that, at that time, Pakistan, India and Dublin specifically, had allocated a number of seats for South African students of colour – students who had no hope of being accepted at any university in South Africa.

This required me to go, personally, to the Ministry of Health in Islamabad. I was advised to hand in my application in person, to highlight my results and try to coerce the officials to, at the least, consider my request. It was the way it was done – the only way to get their attention.

I had completed my Inter-science studies in 1965. I stayed on in Lahore with a friend of mine and then, from Lahore, I took a train to Islamabad. From there we travelled to Rawalpindi. This was a journey that could take anything from three to four hours. I was accompanied by a friend and we had travelled for about an hour when we came to Azeerwahad which is a little station, when we realised that war had broken out between India and Pakistan. And we also learned that the first train that was bombed by the Indian planes was at Wazirabad. We thanked our good fortune. If we had arrived a little earlier, we would have been on the train that was shelled by the Indian Air Force. We saw the people, the dead and the injured, and we saw the shells in the other train and how badly it was damaged.

My friend, who was also my cousin, was with me. There were also some teachers in our coach. An Anglo-Indian guy, who was a teacher at one of the schools out in Rawalpindi, asked us, "What will you chaps do now?" We replied, "We're going to Islamabad." And he says, "There's no way you'll be able to get to Islamabad tonight because there won't be any taxis, you know, there'll be a blackout." And we asked, "What's a blackout?"

Finally, we did get to Rawalpindi and there was a total blackout. Somehow, we managed to get a taxi. The entire city was in darkness because of the air raids. It was impossible to find accommodation. The taxi driver was a pretty decent chap and he took us home to his house and said, "Tomorrow morning you must go to Islamabad," and that was very nice of him. When we entered his home I put on the lights and he said, "What are you doing? You want to get us killed?" I asked, "Why?" and he said, "You know the idea of a blackout is so the aircraft can't see you!"

We slept there overnight. The next morning we took a taxi to Islamabad. We had a friend there who worked in the Health Ministry, though he was a junior clerk there.

So, we were three South Africans staying there with him. His wife worked for an airline, she was an air hostess, so she was not in most of the time. At night, Islamabad being a new city, they did not have siren services so we were then employed – the three South Africans – because we had nothing else to do. They employed us to walk around at night and use huge drums and whistles because everybody was sleeping. So we used to walk around with these huge drums and, as soon as we heard the sirens go off, we blew the whisle and walked around beating the drums so that people could get up and go into the shelters.

We also had to dig a shelter to protect ourselves. The rules were simple: the moment the air raid started, we were to jump into the shelter and place a handkerchief between our teeth, to ensure that if a bomb explodes close to you, you did not accidently bite on your tongue.

Our host, the guy from the ministry, advised us on how to behave.

In the midst of all this, we had our lighter moments too. On one such occasion, we were huddled in the shelter and Corsa, our friend from the Ministry, said something about "this bloody stinking hanky!" We lit a candle and burst out laughing. Corsa had grabbed someone's dirty sock and stuck it between his teeth. It was a hilarious incident, and we laughed about it openly.

Eventually, when things returned to normal, I managed to get admission into the dental school in Hyderabad, which is in Sindh

Province. The college had just been established, and was one of the best in Pakistan.

On completion of my dentistry course I moved on to the medical school in Lahore. This was the King Edward College. After three months, I called it a day. I was repeating the same courses that I had already completed, and decided to revert to dentistry.

When I decided to return to Lahore, four of us rented a nice little apartment. We were all South Africans and we were receiving a reasonable allowance. On occasion, we could afford to eat out at a five-star hotel.

Later we hired a Pakistani cook. We soon realised that this man knew nothing about cooking. His name was Afzal. We had a guy from Krugersdorp who knew a little about cooking, and we had a copy of *Indian Delights* with us. We taught him a little about culinary matters and we paid a reasonable wage. We had a cleaning lady who used to come every morning and sweep the place.

One day the lady decided not to show up and we told Afzal, "You can now also clean the place," and we offered to pay him exactly what we paid the lady. However, he bluntly refused to sweep. Although he was very poor he stated, "Hey, I cannot sweep, you know. I am supposed to be a cook. And so it's below my dignity."

I had bought a motor car and whilst we were washing it, the neighbours came over and said, "How can you wash the car? You need to get servants to do it! You are not supposed to do this job. It is below your dignity!" To maintain our so-called dignity, we discontinued those efforts.

We were then informed that the Pakistani degree would not be recognised in South Africa unless we did a post-graduate course in anatomy. In our naivety, we decided to further our studies privately. We went to the mortuary and told the guy in charge, "We need a body to take home." He was horrified and refused to talk to us. Eventually, with much persuasion and a bundle of money, we obtained possession of a body.

Now it was time to begin dissecting the body and expanding

our knowledge. For us, it was an exercise in education, and we did not see it as the remains of a man. But our cook, who was a pretty decent sort, stumbled on the body and almost lost his mind, shouting and screaming.

We decided to return the body to the mortuary, but the chap in charge refused to take it back unless we paid him what was for that time, a huge sum. We had no choice but to pay up. Our stupidity had almost bankrupted us and it was a good learning curve.

Seven

ADAM: Pakistan gave us enormous exposure. There were far too many patients and nowhere near enough doctors. We were exposed to attending to fractured jaws and that sort of thing; things that a dentist elsewhere would not be expected to do. No other country would allow you to do this. In India and Pakistan you could do that sort of thing, you could experiment.

I recall how insensitive one can become when exploring the human body in the first year. After six to eight months we became quite immune to the dead bodies lying around us. I look back and I think, God, we must have been terrible people.

When I qualified, we were told that the qualification was not going to be recognised in South Africa. I applied to England and was told that it would take two to three years to re-do the degree in England. Alternatively, I could apply to the Royal College of Surgeons, but I would be required to work in a hospital for two years and, of course, no hospital was willing to give us jobs for two years.

I came home to South Africa for a few weeks and went to London to pursue the first part of the course. I knew a Professor Prophet at the UCH College. He was a wonderful man. I had been corresponding with him for the last three years, from my third year onward. And when I went to see him, I found that he was an amazingly warm man, a total gentleman. He was very high up in the dental world and he said he'd try and get me into the college.

He came back to me later to say that he was unable to get me in. Three months down the line, whilst I was at the Royal College of Surgeons in England, he phoned my apartment and said, "I have spoken to my friend Professor Stoy out in Belfast, would you want to go to Belfast?" I said, "Yes, I'll come and see you". I went to see him and he said, "Look, Stoy has accepted you, do you want to go down?" I said, "Yes." He said, "When?" I replied, "Next week," to which he responded, "Why don't you go this week?" I said, "Yes, why not!"

In those days when I sent a telegram – it was all telegrams – to inform the family at home saying that I was going to Belfast, they objected quite strongly, "No, Belfast is too dangerous." I told Professor Prophet about the family's concerns and then I said, "Look, I don't mind whether you send me to Timbuktu," (which was interesting as I later became involved with the Timbuktu manuscripts which enlightened me to one of the oldest Muslim civilisations).

So, I went to Belfast. There were no non-whites there at the time, and especially no Indians that I knew of and, for once, I felt quite lonely. I was alone, I was scared and I stayed at the YMCA. On my first night, whilst I was sleeping, I had an asthmatic attack. I opened the doors and I thought I was dying. Eventually I drifted off to sleep and the next morning I went to the college and I met the great, quick Professor Stoy. He was Dean of the Dental School and he was an amazing man.

I was in Belfast for about a year and that was a very, very happy period because the Irish are just absolutely wonderful people, especially the Catholics. They were very welcoming. They almost embraced us as brothers. And there were always more Irish women than Irish men, because Ireland was very poor in those days and the only thing that Ireland, Northern and Southern, exported was men. When you went to a dance – oh – you found lots of ladies there. The Irish are beautiful ladies, lovely ladies, so it was a good period in my life, really.

Many of my friends married the Irish ladies. I believe many more of us would have married them but there was the fear that we wouldn't be allowed back in South Africa, because of apartheid. Those who did marry had to stay in Ireland or make lives for themselves elsewhere and not in South Africa. In that sense, it was a form of exile.

When I had told Professor Prophet that I would go even to Timbuktu, I did not even know where Timbuktu was, I actually thought that it was a place that didn't exist. And the strange part is that I was later involved with saving the Timbuktu manscripts. It's amazing, it was 35 years later before I came to find out where Timbuktu was and how I became involved in Timbuktu.

I then went to Edinburgh for a short while, and sat for the exams for the Royal College of Surgeons. When I got my degree from the Royal College of Surgeons, I went to London and I practised in London for about a year. It was a wonderful period in my life because suddenly I was a fully qualified dentist and practicing in London. Wow! – London was the top of the world then. It was as if all your dreams had been achieved. It was a dream that I didn't know awaited me.

Life is very strange. It plays with us. My going away to Pakistan was just a little frustration at the time concerning the family business, and for a bit of adventure. There was no definite plan that I would do dentistry, medicine or any other specialist activity. In those days you never went abroad and going abroad was a "wow" thing. Life was what all our desires were about. The travelling, going by plane and the whole idea of studies was all about adventure, seeing the world. The studies were an excuse. So, therefore, sometimes I feel that I have qualifed by default.

I was fortunate in that my parents gave me the opportunity to do that and I embraced the opportunity and I put in a lot of hard work, considering that after nine years in business my brain was almost cooked. When you go into business you're running on the subconscious mind, but not doing anything truly creative. I was not confident enough to go into studies like medicine and dentistry at that time, and when we met doctors and dentists they were like gods to us, or demi-gods, and we always thought that for them to do medicine and dentistry or any other profession, they must be intellectuals of note.

I very quickly learned that that was not true. Although most professionals I meet are very good at their jobs, but even those that are brilliant and excellent at their job, know very little besides their own area of speciality. They are not necessarily intellectual and they are not people of the world. They know very little of philosophy, many of them do not know art or poetry. It is all an exterior projection that we project on how smart the guy must be.

It's like, when talking of people with lots of money, we say, "Wow, he's got lots of money so he must be smart," but more often it is being in the right place at the right time and just putting in lots of work.

London was a good place to be in and I had my own little apartment and was earning good money. And the national health system provided a lot of exposure. I worked in several practices in London. I did lots and lots of locums in the South East, South West, North West, North East and, therefore, I had a pretty good knowledge of the country. At the time, I think I was better orientated in London in terms of geography than I was of any major city in South Africa. London was, at that time, the heart of the world.

Of course, New York was too, but London was still THE place to be. In the English-speaking world there were only two places to be: London and New York. New York was too far away to even dream or think about. All we had was London – England and London. Probably because we were part of the Commonwealth and we were so closely associated with the country that London was always easy to live in.

For purposes of study, London was the place. Most South Africans would want to study in London, never in the States, because I suppose we adopted a lot of English ways and England had a footprint out in Africa, especially South Africa. So yes, my studying in London and working in London was a great time for me. And, in a way, it was an indication that I had been successful in life. I do not know whether that is strictly true but everybody, including the major universities here, would think highly of you if you have had experience in London.

And I had an added advantage: I had also lectured at the New Cross Dental Auxiliary School. That served me well in later years. Being teachers, we were students in a way because, as we were imparting knowledge, we were imbibing a lot from the students as well as the professors that were on a full-time basis there.

And, finally, like all good things, London came to an end.

Eight

NOORJEHAN: It was at this time that Adam came along and "rescued" me. He was en-route to another Transvaal dorp to see a girl there with a view to marriage. He had stopped by at his sister's place who lived in our town. She insisted that he see me while he was there. She telephoned my mother and told her she was bringing her brother over for tea that afternoon and I heard my mother say a silent prayer, "Dear Allah, make it right this time." Whether it was her prayer or whether it was fate, it is said among our people that each of us is born with his or her soul mate. Adam was my soul mate.

He came to tea with his sister. They were comfortably settled in our lounge. I was to take in the tea, but at the last moment my courage failed me. What if he did not like me? My mother had invested so much in this visit. Although the visit was at such short notice, she had gone into circles of frenzy and put out elaborate snacks for tea. The visitors couldn't be kept waiting, so my sister, in exasperation, took in the tea. Adam declined the tea. He wanted milk. My sister returned and thrust the glass of milk in my hand. "You see to your baby!" she said, "I have done my duty."

I walked in with the milk and gave it to Adam, too embarrassed to raise my eyes and take a good look at him. What little I saw pleased me. Adam, for his part, inspected me from top to toe. He obviously liked what he saw for later in the afternoon, his sister invited us to her home. Her brother, she said, wished to speak to me. So the three of us, my mother, sister and I, went to her house. We were led into the main lounge, but very soon the others retired to the adjoining "ladies lounge", and Adam and I were left alone.

We mumbled something to each other and then I surprised both of us, "How come you're a dentist and you are wearing

45

dentures?" I asked. That broke the ice. He burst out laughing and I joined in. We talked for the brief time our elders allotted us, and in that time, strange as it seems, we discovered a compatibility that attracted us to each other.

Two weeks later, Adam contacted my brother Solly and suggested we meet at his niece's house in Balfour, his hometown, where he was attending a wedding. We met privately and he proposed to me personally.

He said he was attracted to me and wished to marry me, and if I agreed, he would send a formal proposal to my family. But he warned me that his family would always come first and if I accepted his proposal, I would have to accept that. At that time, I did not see how I could take preference over his family. He had lived with his family all his life; I was a perfect stranger. I nodded acceptance.

Romance had never been a part of the other proposals. I didn't expect romance in this one either. I understood marriage to be a relationship between two families rather than two persons. It never crossed my mind to question Adam's allegiance to his family and I gave no thought at all to the fact that he was giving me a minor role in our marriage, or that he was bringing his family into it as the important consideration.

Then he told me he had spent many years living in London and that he had had a relationship with a young woman. That discouraged me. "Why then are you not marrying her?" I asked.

He replied that for reasons far too complex for him to explain and for me to understand: "If I had wanted to marry her, I would have," he said. "Marriage was not part of our relationship and that relationship has ended."

He then took my hands and looked into my eyes and I felt a trembling within me and realised that I loved the man and definitely wanted to marry him.

We were formally engaged and enjoyed a short courtship. Adam was a most attentive suitor. He telephoned regularly and over some weekends drove all the way from Durban to be with me. Those were quite the best days of my life. All too soon the engagement period ended and we were married, on Settlers Day.

A good day, I thought, to "settle" into our new life. Ours was a low-key wedding, since I had lost my grandmother only a month before and it would have been unseemly to enter into a lavish celebration so soon.

We spent our wedding night at Adam's parental home in Balfour and left the next day for Durban, as Adam had to get back to work. We had no time for a honeymoon. Anyway, a honeymoon was not part of our tradition and never entered our minds.

Adam's warning that his family came first was soon upon me. Within six weeks of our marriage, I was heavily involved with a part of his family. One evening, while we were having dinner with my sister, Sheila and her in-laws, we were alerted by a telephone call. Adam's brother, his four children and their nanny had arrived and we had to hurry home and settle them in. I did just that and proceeded to be the perfect hostess.

At that time, we were living in rented premises and in the process of moving into the house Adam had bought, during our engagement. My duties as a housewife descended upon me like a whirlwind. I was eighteen, and unused to housework. Being the ace shop assistant, I had been spared those chores. Now I found myself cooking, cleaning, entertaining and moving house all at once. Nobody paused to think for a second how I was coping or whether I was coping at all. I was a married woman and, as such, I was expected to cope and get on with it. They were only interested in results, not in the struggle that preceded these results. I am pleased to say that I turned out to be a very competent housewife. I ran a beautiful home and gave stunning parties, prepared gourmet dishes, but realised that I had become accomplished through the most nerve racking experiences of trial and error and high tension. Under those circumstances I always questioned myself. Did I do right? Was I a failure? Would I get by? I watched Adam and his family put the first morsels of food in their mouths and waited for their reaction, my own mouth plugged by my heart. I used to wait until dinner was done with a sigh of relief, but only after they left the table, satisfied. Then and then only did my heart unplug itself from my mouth and descend to its customary place.

Our home was not just ours; it was also Adam's family home. He owed so much to his family; they had put him through his studies and set him up in his practice. I loved and respected his family. I did whatever I could for them and strove to live up to their demands and Adam's expectations. I was so anxious to please and be a good wife and a good daughter-in-law that I never paused a moment to think what all this anxiety was costing me.

Adam bought me a car and that gave me a sense of independence but also added to my responsibilities as I was now expected to do the shopping, that Adam had done before.

Nine

ADAM: My return home was also the facing of a new reality. When I arrived home, I more or less knew what the scope was for dentistry, but my dad advised me to open in Lenasia, the Indian township near Johannesburg. I said, "Okay."

I was only the second non-white dentist in the Transvaal, and I had gone up to Lenasia to find a place with gravel roads and buckets for toilets. It repelled me. I said, "No, that's not where I want to practise." So then I thought, "Maybe I should go to Cape Town." I learned that there were only two or three non-white dentists there but I was put off by the long distance from Balfour, and I did not want to stay in Cape Town. I decided it was too far away from home, from which I had already been away for too long!

Then I explored P.E. and the non-European hotel, The Alabama. I was, fortunately, introduced by a friend of mine from Durban to seek out a friend of his in Port Elizabeth, and this friend then invited me – they had a doctors' "get together" during the time I was there. There were about ten or fifteen doctors and specialists. I remember this because before this meeting, I went to see the only non-white dentist in P.E., Dr Moodley, to get some idea as to what the scope was out there. When I got there he had a queue, almost like a bus queue. When I finally spoke to him, he said, "Well, you know the scope isn't great out here." And I thought to myself, "Well, and yet he's so busy."

So, when I attended the meeting, I spoke to these doctors. I also remember a coloured gentleman among them who was an orthopaedic surgeon. He asked me where I was staying. When I told him, he said I should stay at a five star hotel. It was 1972 and I was sure non-whites were off limits in a five-star hotel.

But, anyway, when we got down to talking to these people at the doctors' meeting, they were somehow trying to convince me to set up a practice in P.E. They explained that I would get lots of medical aid patients and that they would also refer patients to me. In addition, they pointed out that I could easily contract my services to the huge motor industry.

I couldn't help wondering why they were so helpful and keen for me to practise there. With a bit of hesitation, I plucked up my courage and asked, quite bluntly, "Why are you guys so keen to convince me to stay?" "Because we need your services," one of them replied, equally bluntly. He was a coloured guy and a thorough gentleman, "Dr Moodley can't attend to everybody, he is far too busy. Our people are living in pain. Having you here would be a blessing!"

When I pointed out that Dr Moodley was of a different opinion, I was told: "He is only doing extractions and minor dental work. We need fillings, crowns and root canal work done on us. The white dentists here are not keen to attend to us. This forces us to go to Cape Town for treatment. You could save us from all that."

This was all very encouraging, but I was keen to see what the scope in Durban was like. It ended up being the best move I had ever made. Strolling along Grey and Victoria Streets, reminded me of India and I felt at home.

I brought my dad along because he was not quite convinced that I would be able to make a living in dentistry amongst the Indian population. My dad said, "You've qualified now, you know, are you going to charge only a few shillings for an extraction, we may even have to support you." My father did not know that there's much scope in dentistry and a lot more to do besides extractions.

And, finally, I set up practice in Chatsworth. And when I started the practice I had very small premises. A cousin of mine managed to get me these premises and I was in the heart of Chatsworth, which was a very popular shopping area – there were very few shopping areas in Chatsworth in those days. And immediately, I got quite busy. We used to start at eight o'clock in the morning and only finish at six o'clock in the evening.

I was then in my thirties and I decided that it was time I had a permanent companion to share my life with. My friends introduced me to suitable ladies, and they took me to houses where there were unmarried girls. At the time I had a friend by the name of Moosa Gani, a wonderful man, who always accompanied me on these excursions. He was a very likeable man, extremely popular and had an entrée to the best of families in Durban.

I was aware that this was not the best way of going about it. I was of the opinion that two people contemplating a permanent relationship needed to date for a while, and get to know each other. But, this was the way it was done in those days and I simply followed the rules. With prospects in Durban looking bleak, I went to the Transvaal.

I was introduced to several young ladies by my sisters and my cousins. One weekend, as I was going to Potchefstroom where my sister lives, she told me she was going to Mafeking, to see a particular young lady. As I was about to leave, my sister from Middelburg phoned me (my eldest sister), and insisted that I go to her place immediately. When I told her I was about to leave for Mafeking, she said, "Listen, don't worry about that. Just come here. I've got the right person for you."

I ended up going to Middelburg and my sister took me to meet a girl by the name of Noorjehan. When we got there, Noorjehan's sister came over to serve tea and samoosas. At the time I didn't drink tea, and so I said, "No, I don't drink tea, I'm going to have milk." I think the lady looked a little annoyed by my peremptory response. The sister went back and told Noorjehan to serve me herself and added: "They expect us to parade like cattle in a showground."

I overhead the comment, and sat up in anticipation. Noorjehan had no option but to attend to us herself. When she walked in with the tea tray, she tossed her head, looked at me disdainfully, and with a touch of anger, deposited the offerings on the coffee table. And then, without giving me a second look, she flounced off.

I recall thinking at the time, "Well now, a spirited girl and somewhat independent!" I liked that, and my interest was aroused. And, to my surprise, she had brought me milk. I couldn't help assuming that perhaps, just perhaps, she liked what she saw.

Back at my sister's place I said that I would like to meet that girl again. I needed to talk to her privately and get to know her better. To this day, I don't know how my sister managed to arrange it, but the same afternoon Noorjehan came over, accompanied by her mother.

I had this image of myself, that I was a man of the world, that I had travelled to foreign lands and had met many women. A simple country girl would not throw me off balance. Imagine my surprise, then, to find that for once **I was tongue-tied!** I couldn't think of a thing to say, my mind was in a whirl. I just looked at her wordlessly, my head spinning. And then I heard her ask, "Are you wearing dentures?"

I was taken by surprise and could only mumble, "Yes. How did you know?" When she just smiled and leaned back, I thought: this is ridiculous. I'm behaving like a schoolboy. And then she laughed, softly and musically, and the ice was broken. After that we couldn't stop talking.

I went up to Middelburg every weekend, and courted her with a passion. She was an amazing person, a literary fanatic who read a book a night. And she wrote to me regularly, displaying a terrific command of the language. In that, she was far better than I was. Those were, in some ways, the best years of my life.

After six months of courtship, I proposed and Noorjehan accepted. We married and I brought her to Durban, to a house that I had rented in Merebank. A little later I bought a house in Isipingo Hills. It was a sparkling new house but we soon found out, after the first rains, that the water seeped into the property and made our lives miserable. Somehow, we managed to cope and Noorjehan never held it against me personally for my bad choice in buying this property.

At around the same time I bought a huge bed, with a canopy decorated in garish colours. In my elation, I failed to notice Noorjehan's disgust at the orange and green contraption. But she didn't complain and actually hugged me for being so considerate.

And then, ever so gently, she asked, "Adam, do you mind if I take over the decoration of our house?" That was the first time I realised what a horrendous choice I had made in choosing the ghastly bed.

I immediately agreed to the request but couldn't resist asking her why she hadn't pointed out my bad taste right from the beginning. Noorjehan chuckled, then grinned widely, "Look, Adam, you're the guy with all the fancy degrees, you've lived in London, Edinburgh, Pakistan. I simply accepted that you would have great taste."

It was my turn to laugh. And I gracefully conceded. I was amazed at her exceptional ability to convert our humble home into a tastefully furnished residence.

Ten

NOORJEHAN: Three months after our marriage, Adam decided that we should start our family. The decision had barely sunk in when I found myself pregnant. We had by then moved house and I was finding great pleasure in decorating it. I discovered I had quite a flair for interior decorating. Adam was so pleased with my efforts and proudly showed off my talents to his friends.

The completion of home decoration coincided with the date of my delivery.

I was awakened on Saturday morning, 3rd of August 1974, to terrible labour pains. I packed my overnight bag and left for St Aidan's Hospital.

We reached the hospital and Adam went to see if he could locate any doctors. In those days there were few non-white gynaecologists, and they were terribly busy, so it was always difficult finding them.

I was wheeled into the delivery room. Adam had spoken to the doctors and to the gynaecologist and he was told that he could not stay around, as they did not have private cubicles for birth but had two or three rooms that were quite large where all the women giving birth slept. The only thing that was separating them was curtains and therefore it would have been very awkward for the other women having a non-gynaecological man present there.

The nurse gave me an enema. I had never had an enema before. I recoiled in distaste and horror at what I can only describe as an assault on my body. I found myself running to the loo. Then the nurses said that my waters hadn't broken and that they would have to induce birth. I didn't know what that meant. I knew nothing about "waters" and when they began to prod me, I shrank away from them, cowering and retreating. "What are they doing to me?" I thought, "I have only come to have my baby.

What is all this?" I suddenly began to feel terribly alone. I was a taut bundle of nerves and was forced to abandon myself to their mercy. I started to cry, because I didn't know what was happening and what would happen. The nurses were scolding me and ordering me about. In the midst of this, the doctor arrived, examined me, and pronounced me ready for delivery.

"Relax!" he commanded, "And work with me. Push as I tell you, as if you were pushing for a bowel movement."

I had come to give birth to my baby. I started to wonder what all this talk about passing a bowel movement was.

I found the analogy disgusting. Yet I pushed, and pushed and the doctor urged me on and on. Suddenly, the doctor's voice changed and he gave a cry of pain. Something had happened to his back; I was left alone to push, which I did, tearing myself. The baby was too big and the doctor had not prepared me for that. I felt I was in a slaughter house. Eventually, the doctor returned and at last the baby came. The doctor left prematurely after the delivery to attend to his back once again. He forgot to instruct the nurses to stitch me. No one brought me my baby and I didn't ask for it. I was too exhausted and in too much pain. I was bleeding profusely.

It was several hours before I was moved to the theatre to stop the bleeding and to be stitched up. I was at last moved to my ward which was full of people but I could recognise no one. My vision was blurred due to the blood I had lost. Finally, the baby was brought to me. "It's a girl," Adam whispered, standing over me. I was too feverish to respond and an infection had set in. It was a drip and blood transfusions for me over the next few days. I took no joy in Shamima. I was in no condition even to hold my little girl.

After a week I came home with the baby. I looked at myself in the mirror and could barely recognise the gaunt face I saw. I had lost a lot of weight. I looked at my child in despair. How would I manage? I was weak; the fever had not yet left me, and the baby required attention. We hadn't bonded, Shamima and I. We were apart emotionally, and I was in no condition to be a mother to her.

I found this unnatural; I worried about it and went into bouts of weeping. I didn't know how to be a mother. What were my relatives thinking of me? What was Adam thinking of me? The baby was now my responsibility. I struggled with Shamima's routine and eventually got it right. Where knowledge failed, instinct took over. It was a struggle but Adam thought I was managing and his opinion mattered above all to me. About three months after her birth, I went into post-natal depression without recognising it. I collapsed. I could do nothing. I was content to leave the baby with others. Neither Adam nor I could understand my behaviour. I would break into bouts of crying, became listless and incapable of attending to the housework or the baby. Adam helped me with both the baby and the housework but not in the presence of others out of fear of being called the wife's servant, "*Bibi ka goolam*". This was the attitude that our community at the time displayed – a man was not a man unless he behaved in keeping with certain rigid conventions. Adam, unconventional and deeply caring, dismissed them with a shrug of his shoulders. I was petrified of being alone.

I became desperate. I began to see myself as a failure both as a mother and as a wife. I was useless, I thought, and the more I destroyed myself, the more depressed I became.

Adding to my depression was our house. It had been purchased on account of its low-lying terrain to facilitate my mother-in-law's mobility in her wheelchair. But each heavy rainfall flooded the house. Draining the water and wiping the floors and then living for weeks with the putrid, damp smell drove me crazy. I just felt hopeless and helpless.

I would have continued in this state, without help, had Adam not diagnosed my condition as depression. He had a patient who was a female anaesthetist and who told him that she had had similar symptoms after giving birth. Her husband, a surgeon, had told her that she was just being difficult but she told Adam that she had gone into post-natal depression after the birth of her baby. Adam was convinced that I was suffering from the same malady and he took me to a psychiatrist. It was a relief that the psychiatrist understood my bouts of crying and did not dismiss my condition as just childish behaviour, as the people around me were doing. The only disadvantage was that he prescribed powerful drugs to bring me out of the depression. Those drugs had their own side-effects, but they succeeded in restoring me to a semblance of normality, albeit at a high emotional cost.

People around me, mostly Adam's relatives and mine, didn't believe in post-natal depression. I had the feeling that they were thinking that I could control my behaviour and that I was just badly behaved. Psychiatrists help only up to a point; it is then left to you to help yourself and your capacity to do so depends on the support you get from your immediate family. I had practically no support from that quarter. Indeed, in some respects it was quite the opposite.

The house kept flooding and I could never get used to the stench of damp carpets. I went about my duties wordlessly, never complaining, always trying to be a good wife, a perfect daughter-in-law. I bottled up all my resentment and that, I believe, in retrospect, is in part the root of my present problems.

My depressive state continued for a year; I gradually recovered from it and began to take an interest in my daughter. We then began the journey of discovering each other and finding joy in each other's company.

Shamima had just turned two when I found myself pregnant again. Adam was pleased; I was frightened. The ordeal of my first delivery was still vivid in my mind.

Humeira was born healthy and hearty and fortunately there were no problems with her delivery.

On Humeira's first birthday, Adam announced that we were leaving for the UK. He had had enough of his practice and had decided to specialise. We would be moving to London, I was quite surprised and shocked. I tried to dissuade him because I thought that he had built an excellent practice and would be better off just tending to that for the next couple of years. However, he was quite determined that he needed to specialise and, over a period of time, I fell in with his plan.

I was quite disconcerted and very frightened at the prospect of leaving my new-found comfort zone amongst friends and family in Isipingo. It was like uprooting for the unknown. It was a big step to take. I had been abroad only once and that was on a holiday. Making a home in a foreign country is quite different. And, to make things worse, we were taking everything with us, including some of the household stuff: pots, pans, etc. And there was the added chore of having to sell our house and the surgery. There was so much to do in so short a period. We were planning to leave within the next six months.

It took us all of that time to wind up our affairs in Durban. Adam then flew off to London, whilst I went to my mum's place in Middelburg, and I would join him once he had secured accommodation for us in London.

Whilst at my parents' home in Middelburg, Humeira, my second-eldest daughter, had an ear infection. We were due to fly off to London in a few days, and I decided to have her examined by a doctor. He confirmed my fears and decided that the quickest solution would be an injection.

Humeira had never before been treated with penicillin, in any form. I was still chatting to the doctor when she started pounding my chest with her little fist and clenching her teeth.

I immediately brought this strange behaviour to the doctor's attention. It was obvious to me that she was having an adverse reaction to the medication. We rushed her to a hospital where they decided that she had to be placed in an oxygen tent. Humeira bluntly refused to enter the tent unless I went in with her.

This was my child, I loved her dearly. I had no choice but to comfort her, to join her in the cramped space and hold her hand. For the next twenty four hours I did not sleep. The paramount thought, in all that time, was that a lack of oxygen for a certain period leads to brain damage. I hoped that we had got her to hospital in time.

All I could do was look at her and pray. God heard my prayer and Humsie came out of it, normal and, once again, full of herself. However, this was during the height of apartheid. My daughter needed to visit the bathroom urgently.

I had to take her to the non-white section, and when she saw the hole in the ground she cringed and refused to go. In desperation, I turned to the sister-in-charge. Although the poor dear was in danger of losing her job and in fear of her colleagues, she took us to the white section and my daughter was finally able to relieve herself.

We had to spend the night in the hospital, so that the doctors could observe her progress. I was still anxious about my little girl and stayed with her. I was forced to sleep in the tent and I spent the night watching a troop of ants going about their business in an orderly manner, several of them rolling a single grain of sugar. I was fascinated by the meticulous way in which they worked, almost with military precision.

When we were back home, I called Adam to explain what had happened. He was considerably upset, but I reassured him that Humsie was fine.

Eleven

NOORJEHAN: A few days later, I was on my way to the UK. What was normally a twelve hour flight, for some inexplicable reason, perhaps because of bad weather, became a tedious journey that took all of twenty-four hours.

I made my children as comfortable as possible. A young couple, in the seats behind me, were observing me closely. Finally the husband stood up and complimented me on my children's good behaviour. He added that he was hoping to start a family of his own, but his wife was reluctant to do so as she feared that she would be unable to cope.

I had a quiet chat with the wife and said that, whilst her fears were justified, having children was not as bad as she thought. For the duration of the trip, we chatted about it and I'm sure I allayed most of her fears, explaining that children cement a marriage and provide a bond that lasts for a lifetime.

Pretty soon we landed, and, in the bustle of the airport, we lost sight of each other, without exchanging names and addresses. I often wonder if they eventually did have children, and whether my reassurances may have had anything to do with it. I do not believe in coincidence. I believe that our paths crossed through some divine purpose. I like to think that I had done the correct thing.

I loved London. It seemed to me that, in winter, the dawn and sunset simply collapsed into each other and light disappeared. After two lovely years we returned to South Africa. Adam opened a surgery and asked me to assist him. I accepted eagerly.

Suddenly, I was very busy: running the house, caring for my daughters, and helping at the surgery. And, to add to all that, we decided to build a house. I was in charge of its completion. As if all this was not enough, I was pregnant once again, for the third time.

I was, for once, very fortunate. The pregnancy proceeded well and the delivery was a dream. Not long after Nadia was born we moved into our new home. My life was complete: I had three beautiful daughters, a husband who loved me and was an excellent provider, and was adored by both our extended families.

Nadia, a bubbly and happy child, was "adopted" by a couple who were very dear friends of ours. Vasie and Hoosen had married across the religious divide, and this had caused a bit of friction between their respective families. So, Adam and I were both happy to provide a pleasant diversion, and, of course, Nadia loved the attention.

Our little girls were angels, they doted on each other and gave us such pleasure as we had never dreamed possible. And as they grew, their personalities flowered. We marvelled at how different they were from each other, and how distinct they were as individuals. Watching them at play, and listening to their laughter, was like participating in a song of love and devotion.

Shamima fitted into the elder sister role quite naturally. No one had to teach her, or direct her. She was protective of Nadia almost from the moment she was born, and mothered Humeira when I was not around. Shamima became more and more my companion, offering to help me at every turn and taking an interest in cooking at an early age. She spent time with me in the kitchen, helping with the salad, peeling potatoes and chatting away. She felt grown up and saw herself as my confidante, as indeed she was growing into. She was shy, demure, quiet and, given the opportunity, she would withdraw into a corner with a book or spend hours before the television.

Nadia copied practically everything Shamima did and wanted to be just like her. She would offer to make tea when visitors came and, on one occasion, I absentmindedly accepted her offer. To our surprise – Vasie and Hoosen were with us on that occasion – she wheeled in the tea trolley with tea, cups and biscuits. She had inveigled the housekeeper into making it for her.

Humeira was the funny one. She said and did things that often sent us off into peals of laughter. Once we were watching a soapy, and there was a somewhat steamy love scene. Shamima looked away embarrassed, but Humsie commented, "They are making *maja*," (having fun) and that broke the embarrassment, and we laughed and laughed till the tears rolled down our cheeks. She was my shadow, forever following me around.

Adam and I never celebrated Valentine's Day, but for the girls, it became a day of showering gifts on their teachers. The other children bought expensive gifts. We picked flowers from our garden and made them into pretty presentations.

There was a time when Nadia wanted a Christmas tree, and that became an issue between Adam and I. Adam thought we would be confusing the girls by introducing mixed religious symbols. I was all for indulging my daughter. I bought her a little white Christmas tree and put it in Nadia's room.

Adam was a fun father. The girls looked forward to his return home from work. They appeared never to have enough surfaces on their bodies for him to kiss.

"Such wet blubbery kisses," Nadia would say.

"You don't want them?" Shamima would retort. "I'll have your share as well," and Adam would pretend to be offended and turn away and say, "My three angels don't want me so I'll go to Balfour and get myself three angels from there." The girls would then protest and cry and slap him and he would gather them in his arms and the kissing would start all over again.

Hide and seek was a favourite game. Daddy would have to search and pretend that he could not find them and then, as they thrilled in anticipation, he would pounce on them and they would scream and laugh and ride on his back.

Adam surprised the girls when we returned from a holiday with my parents. He had built them a miniature cycling track with a cement road and all the traffic markings. They were keen cyclists at the time. He also built us a swimming pool in the garden and the girls became skilful swimmers. I loved watching our daughters dive and splash and emerge like seals, race each other, glide like mermaids and then turn on their backs and swim backstroke. The pool filled up on some days with their friends and I loved the sound of the children's laughter as it filled our house and garden.

I had strong ideas about raising my daughters. There were relatives who thought I was too stern with them. There were relatives who said I was stingy because I didn't overstock their wardrobes with unnecessary dresses. My girls had as many dresses as they needed. I was against indulging them and sought to discipline them and inculcate moral values that would serve them well in their adult lives. I disapproved totally of the many affluent parents who plied their children with material luxuries to make up for the time they couldn't spend with them, and to overcome their guilt. I have no regrets at all that I didn't indulge my daughters. I did what I believe to be the best for them.

There were the usual parties on their birthdays, the presents and the balloons. Eid came and brought its joys and the girls revelled in their new clothes, their pockets filled with cash which they spent on buying small luxuries for themselves. They joined me in prayer, spreading their prayer rugs alongside mine, their little forms covered in veils.

When Nadia was born, Shamima and Humeira were already at school. School was fun, *Madressa* an agony. I discovered this painfully several months later after I had enrolled them. I sensed that they feared going to *Madressa*, although they never complained and went dutifully. It wasn't long before I discovered the cause for their anxiety. I had been through it myself. *Molvis* are notorious for the corporal punishment that they mete out to their pupils. I was shocked that the situation had not changed, that they still used serpents, devils and the cane to intimidate their charges, and hadn't yet learnt to use love.

I would have remained ignorant of the situation had I not noticed a lump on Shamima's head one morning whilst combing her hair. I was appalled when she told me that the Moulana had hit her. I discovered that he did this regularly to all the children. He hit them with a cane on any convenient part of their bodies. I was enraged. I drove to the Moulana's house and there and then warned him that if he touched my daughters ever again, I would withdraw them from his *Madressa*. He didn't appear to care very much. He said that he had to discipline the children and if I wanted my daughters to grow up without discipline, he would spare the rod. I told him that I would discipline them, that was my responsibility, not his.

I could see that things had not changed and the girls continued to fear the *Madressa* though they said nothing. Shamima was wetting her bed and having nightmares about snakes. Then one night, Humeira started screaming and I found her cowering under the blanket and shaking. I took her in my arms and cradled her. Did you have a bad dream? I asked.

"No, no, no," she sobbed. "I will burn in Hell. The Molvis Sahib said so. He said I was naughty, full stop, I'll burn in hell." I clasped her to my heart. I kissed away her tears. I soothed her. "You will never burn in hell, you are an angel. You will go to heaven." But, she insisted that she would go to hell. The Molvis Sahib had told her so.

I was enraged. I drove to the Molvis's house and banged on the door. He saw me and feared my anger and so he shut the burglar gate on my face. He thought I would attack him physically. I shouted at him and told him that he would never see my girls again. I was withdrawing them from his *Madressa*.

The *Jamaat* came to see us. Adam, knowing how incensed I was, did not allow me to speak to them. I wanted to give them a piece of my mind, to tell them that the Molvis knew nothing about teaching children with love. Allah was not a bogey man waiting to catch children and throw them into hell when one of them had offended Him or the Molvis. Allah was love and compassion and mercy. I would not allow such misrepresentation of both Allah and Islam. I would never expose my children to the terror tactics of the Molvis. Adam, aware of my impending anger and outburst, protected the *Jamaat* from it. This I resented.

After this incident, I saw to it that my children did not remain deprived of Islamic education. We engaged a private tutor and everyone was happy. By the end of the year there was a private school which incorporated Islamic education with the secular. I was never in favour of private schools, but this one was different. I wanted my girls to have a good Islamic foundation, to be well grounded in Islamic history and theology and to understand the value of giving (*zakaat*) and recognizing all humanity as one under the ascendancy of the Supreme Being (*Tawhid*). I wanted them to have a strong sense of their own identity and I wanted them to be rooted in faith in the Divine Benefactor so that they would never be in a position of being lost souls.

The new school also spared them from having to attend two school sessions and left them with more free time for themselves.

Apart from the incident at the *Madressa*, our lives moved on an even keel and our happiness continued.

I wanted to give our girls everything that I did not have. They did ice ballet, ice skating and other sport. Humsie liked art, and was very much of a nature person. We got a private tutor for her to help develop her talents. Initially, they did not like the music lessons we organised, but I saw Shamima starting to show an interest and she was playing *Chariots of Fire* fairly well. My days were filled with school and extra-curricular activities, ferrying the children to and from home to the various activities they engaged in. Our lives were full of fun, laughter and song. How were we to know that the devil was lurking in the background?

Twelve

ADAM: About eighteen months from the day of our marriage, Noorjehan gave birth to Shamima. During the delivery, Noorjehan had hurt herself and had to have thirteen stitches, and that really depressed her for a little while, and it took her some three to six months to recuperate. Three years later, we had Humeira and Noorjehan was now the happiest woman in the world. She had a lovely house, my practice was doing well, she was the mother of two lovely daughters and we had some wonderful friends. Being the first dentist in our area I was well respected. Everything was going for us.

However, I must somewhat ruefully confess that men tend to believe that wives are a form of property. We own them. We don't give them the respect they require, nor do we compromise. We assume that we know it all. Although we were very happy together, I felt that I was superior to her in some ways. What I didn't know at the time was that Noorjehan was far wiser and a much better person than I could ever hope to be.

Noorjehan, ever so gently, taught me the finer things in life. Up until then, I found it difficult to hold her hand in public, could not hug her in the presence of other people, and indeed, found it impossible to even gently peck our female friends on the cheek.

In my arrogance, I believed that real men don't do those things. Noorjehan, who was deeply perceptive, quietly but persuasively led me by the hand and introduced me to the sensitive nature of communicating with our friends. She inculcated into me a sense of **feeling** when dealing with people. More than anything, I learned the importance of "touch" and its healing power.

After some five years in practice, I was doing very well indeed. Notwithstanding my success, I had a fervent urge to specialise. And that meant going to London.

To Noorjehan's dismay, I sold the practice and prepared to realise my dream. In fairness to her, she was extremely supportive. That was when I fully appreciated the depth of her love for me.

Initially, I went to London on my own, to look for an apartment. I wanted Noorjehan at my side, and I missed the kids. I was, as always, thinking only of myself. I didn't, not even for a brief moment, consider the consequences of my decision and its effects on Noorjehan.

The family finally came to London. We bought a house, settled down and, instead of specialising, I managed to buy a practice at a very reasonable price and I started practising once again.

Noorjehan was very lonely at first but she soon made friends and, once more, the rafters were ringing with the sounds of laughter and joy. And that was entirely due to Noorjehan's efforts. I realised then, that on my own, I wasn't much good at socialising.

And after about a year or a year and a half, my brother had a kidney transplant, my father was not too well, and so I decided to come back and we returned to South Africa. To this day I'm not quite sure that going to London had been a good move. But Noorjehan was, as always, beside me, quietly leading the way and making the lifesaving decisions. I was quickly learning to follow her wise guidance and appreciating her perspicacity.

Thirteen

NOORJEHAN: In those halcyon days, I laughed a lot and slept a lot. I couldn't, for a moment, imagine that such happiness could ever end. I often marvelled at how good life was: I had a good and loving husband, a comfortable life and three beautiful daughters with impeccable manners. I was so blessed. Shamima was at the stage where we were starting to be companions, having adult conversation, and enjoying mother daughter chit chats. Adam doted on his daughters and they adored him.

We were a very happy and close family – Adam, Shamima, Humeira, Nadia and I.

At this time, there was only one dark cloud in our lives, the illness that had left Adam's mother an invalid in a wheelchair. Adam was very devoted to her and we often went to Balfour to see her over weekends, leaving on Friday or Saturday and returning on Sunday.

At the end of February 1986, one of Adam's cousins telephoned him and said he was concerned about my mother-in-law. He claimed that he had a dream in which Adam's elder brother, Sattar, had come to him and said that the boys were neglecting their mother and she deserved more attention and greater care. That affected Adam badly. He was very close to Sattar, who had died seven months previously of renal failure. Being in Durban, Adam hadn't been able to give him as much attention as he would have liked. He didn't want to live with the same regrets in relation to his mother. He became more anxious to see her.

We decided to visit her during the first weekend in March. We would leave on Saturday and return on Sunday. Adam wanted the children to accompany us on it but I was very unhappy about that.

I suggested that we leave the children behind and that Adam and I fly to Johannesburg and arrange for someone to meet us at the airport. Adam reasoned that it would mean two return trips from Balfour to the airport. Someone would be required to fetch us and then we would have to be dropped off for the return trip. He was, as a result, convinced that we should just drive up.

It was an instinct thing. I was making all sorts of excuses to leave the girls behind: it would be too tiring, they would be fretful and they would miss out on school the next day. Adam said that his mother was really looking forward to seeing the girls and that they should accompany us. I fell in with his plan, reluctantly and rather unhappily. I had this awful, uncomfortable, unexplained, niggling feeling at the pit of my stomach.

_ૐ_

ADAM: I remember it was on a Saturday. My mother was bedridden, and my father had bronchitis and all sorts of illnesses, such as emphysema, etc. I told Noorjehan, "We need to go and see my Mum and Dad." She asked, "You went last week, why should we go again?" I said, "Well, we need to go." Noorjehan added, "Fine, I'll go with you but let's not take the girls along."

Noorjehan was quite insistent about it, "I don't want to take my daughters along." I was keen that we should. She said, "I have a feeling that something is going to happen to us," and then added, "I have a gut feeling, please." And she begged me to reconsider. To this day I regret not listening to Noorjehan. If I had, our lives would have been so different. But "if only" are the words of regret that continue to haunt me. But then I rationalise, and console myself: it happened because it was planned by a higher being – Taqdir, karma, fate, whatever.

I sincerely regret it, but human beings are strange. We relegate our pain to a higher power and we say it was meant to happen. Often, religion and culture help us to cope with these tragic circumstances. The Chinese like to say, "These things happened because the stars were not in our favour, or the planets were not aligned." As Muslims we feel that it's taqdir, it was meant to happen, it does not matter what you did. I needed the philosophy of taqdir, for I could not bear to take responsbility for the disaster, particularly in the face of Noorjehan's insistence that we should not take the children with us. I will have to deal with these nagging "ifs" for as long as I live.

Anyway, we went up to Balfour. Obviously, going to Balfour was a bad omen anyway, because the car got stuck.

ﺞ

NOORJEHAN: Soon it was time to leave for Balfour. I saw to it that the girls were safely buckled in their seats and had sufficient games to keep them occupied, so that they wouldn't grow bored and restless. We picked Adam up at his surgery in Pinetown. Humeira returned to her place at the back and Adam slipped into her vacant seat. He said I should drive while he ate his lunch. A few kilometres later, he took over the driving, commenting that I drove at a snail's pace and goodness alone knew when we would reach Balfour, if we reached Balfour at all at that pace. I didn't mind his sarcasm – I was quite used to it – as it was part of his patronizing, playful attitude towards me.

Our journey continued peacefully, the silence interrupted every now and again by our chatter about odds and ends, nothing serious; and the children's complaints against each other as the one was irritating the other, or the one was not keeping to the rules of the game that they were playing, and finally, it led to one of them refusing to play. On the whole, they were at peace with one another, and if there was some bickering, there was also a lot of loving. They were full of questions about all sorts of things and Shamima, as the big sister, attempted to answer some, but Humeira and Nadia were not satisfied until Mummy or Daddy confirmed her answers.

The car droned on, there were peals of laughter from the back.

I turned around to share in the fun but the children blocked me out. It wasn't my kind of joke they said. I should joke with Daddy. "Silly girls!" I retorted, my pretension at discipline disappearing in my happiness at seeing them so exuberant and in such high spirits.

We were just nearing Ladysmith, a few kilometres away, when the car suddenly stopped. Adam got out and opened the bonnet to examine the engine; it was boiling hot. The radiator was dry and we needed to fill it with water. Not far away there was a small dam and Adam grabbed a container and prepared to head towards it. Shamima wanted to accompany him and the other two chorused that they would also like to go. I said that I need their company as Mummy couldn't be left all alone. So father and daughter carefully squeezed through the fence and were soon sprinting towards the dam. They returned with the water, but that was not the problem. The engine cooled but the car refused to start. What now? There was only one thing we could do: get to Ladysmith, where we had friends, and then deal with the problem there. But how were we all to get us a lift? And what of the car? After much debate, we decided Adam would hike a lift while the four of us "women" waited in the car for his return with a "rescue team".

Adam got a lift from a passing truck and headed towards Ladysmith where he had a friend who owned a bakery. But we didn't have to wait for Adam's return. Friends of ours on their way to Johannesburg saw us and stopped so that we were able to squeeze into their car. Nadia on my lap, Humeira on Shamima's. They dropped us off at Adam's friend's house. His name was Cassim and we were warmly welcomed by Kulsum, his wife. Cassim and Adam had already left to fetch us. I was concerned that they wouldn't find us. Kulsum reassured me that they were sufficiently intelligent to assume we'd got a lift.

Whilst we waited, we spent our time in Ladysmith profitably. Kulsum took us on a conducted tour of the bakery and we watched the bread being prepared for the next morning's delivery. The children were most interested, and especially excited at seeing all the cream cakes! Shamima and I discussed the essay she could write on her return to school: "A Visit to a Bakery".

By now, it was getting dark and there was no sign yet of Adam and Cassim. Kulsum prepared a barbeque for the children. I bathed and refreshed the girls and put them into their pyamas. It was clear we were going to have to travel by night and they should be prepared to sleep in the back seat.

It was well past ten p.m. when Adam and Cassim finally returned. They reported that the car was fine. We then debated as to whether we should return to Durban or continue on to Balfour.

Fate held the trump card. Adam's anxiety about his mother drew us to the conclusion that we should rather carry on to Balfour. So we thanked the Cassims for their wonderful hospitality and proceeded on our journey as planned. Humeira and Shamima were soon asleep in the back seat. Nadia fussed and wanted to be with me, and curled herself in my arms in the front seat, and was soon snoring softly. Like a contented, purring cat.

I gazed on her innocent face. The thought crossed my mind that she was growing up too fast for my liking. She would be five years old on March 20, which was only three weeks away and she was really looking forward to celebrating her party. More importantly, she was looking forward to going to "big school" like her sisters.

I thought how mature Shamima was at ten, having slipped into the big sister role so easily. My post-natal depression period must have made her prematurely independent. It was as if she had told herself in her infancy, "Mummy is not well. I must look after her", and she had done just that despite her tender years.

Humeira, who we ended up calling Humsie, was quite the opposite. She clung to me as if she couldn't have enough of me. Only I was allowed to carry her and only I could wheel her pram. The moment someone took over from me, she instinctively knew, and turned around and protested. She tired me out at times, but mostly I was flattered by her need for me. Now she slept in the back seat, her arms around Shamima. I drew Adam's attention to the twosome at the back of the car, commenting on how sweet they looked in each other's arms. He cast a momentary glance at the back seat and smiled. We were so fortunate in our daughters. I thought of them growing up into three beauties. They had already exhibited their intelligence. They did so well at school.

Shamima and Nadia were healthy – although both were somewhat asthmatic. Nadia was more prone to attacks than Shamima. Humsie had had her problems and the worse was when a car direcly opposite our house hit her. It was during Ramadaan. She had joined us at Sehrie (pre-dawn meal) and insisted on fasting. After much argument we had agreed she could fast half the day. And it was when she was returning home from school on that day that a car knocked her down. We had been worried sick, but she had recovered quite quickly. Besides this accident Humsie had also had a penicillin reaction earlier which almost led to brain damage. This could have led to her becoming a vegetable. Often Adam and I reflected on how she had already survived two major traumatic events, any one of which could have led to her demise.

I sat back in my seat smiling to myself and thought about what they would do when they grew up. Would one of them follow in their father's footsteps and become a dentist? Yes – that would probably be Shamima. She identified most strongly with him. But I wouldn't want her to be a dentist, bending over people's mouths the whole day – so boring and so tiring.

Adam had his dreams for her. He wanted her to spend a year in Pakistan after matric. He had found his own time there very fruitful. It had helped to wean him off his dependency on his family. He often entertained the girls when he related his escapades as a student. Afzal, the students' cook, was their favourite character. They went into peals of laughter when Adam told them how Afzal, when told there would be extra people for dinner, would say, "That's no problem!" and simply add water to the curry. They shivered, their spines tingling with fear when he told them of the time he had bought a cadaver to perfect their knowledge of anatomy, and how Afzal had screamed, and ran like the wind, returning only a week later, during which time they had to do their own cooking. "Serves you right!" the girls used to say, in total sympathy with Afzal.

I wanted the girls to have professions of their own choosing and be independent, but I also wanted them to have lots of fun, to travel, to see the world and enjoy themselves. We would have three sons-in-law, I daydreamed, and grandchildren! Oh, to hold tender, soft babies in my arms again!

Nadia stirred in her sleep and broke into my day dreaming. She was laughing. Adam laughed with her. "She is having a happy dream," Adam commented. The laughter went as suddenly as it had come.

"Adam, what would you like your daughters to be when they grow up?" I asked.

He was very serious as he analysed available opportunities, the various professions and his daughters' aptitudes. He wanted all his daughters to be professionals – doctors or lawyers. Curiously, he didn't give dentistry a thought. We had an animated discussion on our daughters' future. We considered sending them overseas, going to live with them while they studied. The future had so much in store for us, for them.

Fourteen

NOORJEHAN: We reached Balfour as dawn broke, and after sharing warm greetings with the family, went straight to bed. The older girls slept in their own beds, Nadia slept with us.

The next morning, soon after breakfast, we learned that there was going to be a wedding in Balfour that day. The children were most excited, clamouring around our bed with their cousins. Our girls wanted to go to the wedding with their cousins and there was no reason why they shouldn't. I had brought their party dresses with us. I believe in anticipating all eventualities, that's what makes my packing so burdensome.

I helped the girls dress and combed their hair and decorated it with pretty slides. As they went off with their cousins, chatting away, holding hands and laughing in the manner of little girls, I thought that they were the prettiest fairies I have ever seen.

Adam and I used this time to be with his mother, who was at the time staying with her youngest son. She had become completely bedridden, and the sons had been taking it in turns to have her in their homes and care for her.

Before we knew it, the children returned from the wedding. We had lunch and Adam hurried us to get started for Durban. We were packed and ready to leave when suddenly there was a heavy downpour.

"Should we be leaving in this rain?" I asked.

Adam was dubious, but struck a compromise with me. We would drive on to Standerton and if the rain continued we would return to Balfour, sleep the night there and leave early the next morning. Just then there was a clap of thunder and hail began pelting on the roof of the car and on to the windscreen. I looked at Adam. We were packed and ready to leave. We had said our goodbyes. Adam's mother, as usual, had embraced all of us and wept her tears. Adam ignored the hail and started the car.

$$\mathit{ॐ}$$

ADAM: As we drove out of Balfour, it started hailing and Noorjehan said, "Let's turn back." And I replied, "Maybe we will turn back. Let's do about 10 kilometres and, if it doesn't let-up, we'll make a U-turn.

The downpour didn't last. We covered the 50 miles to Standerton in relative comfort. However, I had slept badly the night before and I could feel the waves of fatigue overcoming me.

I considered pulling into a garage and refreshing myself with coffee. It was a fleeting thought, immediately replaced by the knowledge that we wouldn't be served. Those were the apartheid years and, as Indians, a pariah dog was more welcome than we were. So I stopped the car and asked Noorjehan to take over.

I moved into the passenger seat, lowered the backrest and, after throwing a quick glance at my girls – who were all sleeping peacefully – I drifted off into a deep sleep.

$$\mathit{ॐ}$$

NOORJEHAN: When we reached Standerton the rain had stopped and the sun was shining brightly. Adam asked me to take over the wheel. He hadn't slept well and wanted to have his forty winks. Not too long after that, our daughters were up and chatting away aimlessly, idly commenting on the wedding meal, but unanimous in their conviction that the ice cream had been the highlight for all three of them.

As I drove on towards Volksrust, I noticed that they had gone very quiet. I turned my head and found that they were all fast asleep. I was the only one awake in the car. I switched on the radio. Soft, soothing music was soon flowing throughout the car. I lowered the volume to ensure that my family was not disturbed. I checked the speedometer. It registered 120 kilometres per hour. My safety belt was on. I was a confident driver and was used to driving on my own. I had made several trips on this route during the school holidays with the girls. I never fall asleep at the wheel.

We left Standerton, passed by Pardekop, and were heading for Volksrust. There was not much traffic on the road. It was a dual freeway, beautifully tarred with gravel on the sides.

I was humming to the music and tapping my fingers on the steering wheel when, all of a sudden, I felt the car veering to the right and I could not control it. It would not straighten up and continued to the right, onto the opposite side. I screamed out, "Adam, something is wrong. What is happening?" I was in the face of yawning danger. My first instinct was to check for oncoming traffic and give thanks to Allah there wasn't any. In retrospect, I felt that my thanks were premature. The car hit the gravel on the side of the road and seemed to have acquired a will of its own. I pressed my foot hard on the brakes and realised that they were not responding. I cried out to Adam, "We are in trouble!" I screamed, "Adam, help me!"

The car was now spinning completely out of control and there was nothing I could do about it. I felt helpless, when suddenly the car shot up in the air and came back down to a grinding halt. I heard myself calling out to Allah and I heard hysterical screams, not for one moment realising at the time that they were my own. I was overwhelmed by the feeling that something terrible had happened, as indeed it had. I was suddenly aware of my children and started calling for them frantically. There was this sense of uncanny quietness in the backseat, which was soon to be broken by Humsie's moaning and her plea for help. I lunged towards her but found I couldn't reach out to her. "Dear God, what nightmare is this?"

It was no nightmare. I was stuck, locked into my safety belt and couldn't free myself. I couldn't get to my daughter, who needed me. I was trapped.

"Nadia!" I called out frantically.

There was no reply. My screams came back to me like demonic echoes, and all the time I was fighting against the seat belt and kicking at the door like a deranged woman.

Then unexpectedly there was this strange voice, soothing, helpful. The voice was reassuring me. "The children are alright," it said. Then I saw Adam's arm hanging by a ligament and I passed out. When I came to, I heard a voice saying in Afrikaans, "Ons verloor die groot een!" (We have lost the older one). I screamed and pushed with all the strength I could muster. I don't know where it came from, I broke free and was in the back seat with Shamima, cradling her as she took her last breath, and said her last words, "I want to go to school tomorrow!"

Instinct took over where emotion and reason could not cope. I was carrying out the last rite not knowing that I was doing so. I recited the *kalima* and closed her eyes, mechanically and without thought. I had three daughters to worry about but at that moment I was totally focused on Shamima. Somewhere in the back of my mind, I vaguely knew that some good Samaritan had removed Nadia and Humsie to the hospital.

The ambulance arrived. Adam was rolled in and I followed him, screaming for someone to save his arm as he was a dentist and needed his arm to continue working.

ॐ

ADAM: I only came to when the accident happened. Noorjehan aroused me or I woke, unable to register what had happened. I remember I had severe back pains – that's all that I remember. And then there were lots of cars. Somebody took me out of the car and placed me on the grass and said, "Don't move around too much."

There was a nurse, an Afrikaner lady, and I overheard her say to somebody as she put my Shamima next to me, "Sy is weg." ("She is gone.") And I knew that Shamima had passed away. I had no idea what had happened to the other girls, because I was in great pain. All I remember is being taken by ambulance to the hospital. I was drifting in and out of a coma, alternately unconscious and conscious.

꒳

NOORJEHAN: After what felt like an eternity, we reached Volksrust Hospital and Adam was rushed into theatre. I found myself repeatedly asking after Nadia and Humeira. I was told that no children had been admitted to the hospital. I was confused, which was not helped by the fact that Shamima's passing had already numbed me. I was functioning like an automaton. I told the doctor on duty that I had just lost one child and that the other two had been brought to hospital. They were kind enough to check and then informed me that my two children had been taken to the Standerton Hospital. And then they informed me, softly and gently that Nadia was dead and Humeira was fighting for her life. My world stopped. I collapsed to the floor and stared blankly in front of me. I had nothing to live for and then, even as the pain consumed me, I thought of Humeira and I knew that I had to get to her. My mind was screaming that Humeira needed me, and I couldn't understand why they wouldn't take me to her. I had to be admitted first, the nurse insisted, and demanded that I give her the necessary information to complete her form. When I said that my surname was Mahomed, she stopped writing suddenly and, with a strange look on her face, informed me that I was in the wrong section. I was in the part of the hospital that was reserved for Europeans only, and I could not be admitted there. I told her that I didn't want to be admitted. All I wanted to do was to get to my daughter in Standerton.

"But you are in need of medical attention," she mumbled, not quite knowing how to deal with the situation, adding that I needed to go to the Non-European section for treatment.

Adam was still in theatre, in the white section. Shamima was dead, Humeira and Nadia in Standerton. What on earth was I doing here by myself? I was totally lost, desolate, confused and desperate for someone to assist me. Just then I looked up and saw my mother and sister, Ruby. I ran to them and clung to them, sobbing inconsolably. They said that they would take me to Humsie in Standerton but only after I had received the necessary medical attention. I protested as any mother defending her young would. "Who is with Humeira?" I asked.

I had to be there with her, every thread in my body was aching to be there. My mother's instinct was reaching out to protect her, care for and nurture her. I just had to get to her immediately. They took me into their arms and rocked me. They tried to soothe me. I began to fear the worst. Had I lost Humeira too?

"No! No! Dear God, no!" I screamed.

And then my mother reassured me that Humsie was alright.

"You have a lot of wounds that need stitching. They will turn septic. Please! Please! Please!" Ruby begged me, "Trust us".

These were my family, my mother and my sister. Why would I not trust them? But I was a mother too, and I had that mysterious bond to the child I had given birth to. My instincts were aroused and I couldn't accept what they were telling me.

I clung to hope. I began to pray. "Dear God, spare me at least the one child. You have taken away two already, leave me my Humeira. Is that too much to ask for?"

Against all hope, I was clinging to hope. I continued praying feverishly and intensely. I refused to believe that God could abandon me, that He could be so cruel.

I refused to leave the white section of the hospital until Adam was out of the theatre. Finally, they brought him out and he was transferred to the non-white section. Only after that, while I was still drenched in a pool of my own blood, did I agree to let them stitch me up.

I was like a zombie. Everything I was going through was beyond my comprehension.

Adam was still with me, but the girls were gone. I was dead myself, numb and seeing everything as if in a nightmare. I was like a big block of ice – seeing but not feeling.

I kept enquiring after Humeira, and was told that she had

broken both legs and was fighting to survive. And then I heard Adam ask one of his brothers to tell him the truth. I heard him whisper that all my three children had died.

And then my world collapsed. All sense of reality vanished. I ceased to be human. I was reacting like an automaton, like a child's wind-up toy robot. Life had become totally meaningless. I retreated into a mindless void, unable to come to terms with reality.

Fifteen

NOORJEHAN: By now it seemed as though the whole Volksrust community had heard the shocking news and had begun gathering at the hospital. Their presence was restricting movement in the non-European section, causing chaos. I was, by now, out of the theatre. Ruby was beside me, stroking my arm. I could hear myself crying, calling out to my daughters. Adam's brother was talking to him in a low voice, a funereal voice.

I couldn't help thinking that I had no reason to live. I just wanted to die.

Through it all, Adam was a pillar of strength. I could see that he was in deep pain – and that it was not the result of the stitches. He was hanging in there, maintaining a semblance of sanity. Looking at him in the hospital bed, I was shocked by how, literally in a few hours, he had changed so much. His face was drawn, there were lines on his face, lines that had not been there before.

I must have said something, perhaps moaned a little too loudly, when I heard him say, softly and in a defeated voice, "It is God's will. We can only submit to it." Then he added, in Arabic, "*Inna lilla he wa inna ilayhi raa ji oon*" – "From Him we come and to Him we return!"

"No!" I screamed. "No! No! No!" I couldn't accept the finality of it all. There had to be some purpose to life, a reason to be born.

I must have passed out then. When I came to, I was aware that I was in a hospital bed. I had been injected with drugs to assist me in coping with my grief. To the casual observer I appeared outwardly calm, but I was inwardly dead.

Suddenly I was wide awake and I heard the concerned voice of Adam's sister asking where we wanted our daughters to be buried.

Buried? Buried? The words beat at my heart. My little ones buried? Thrown into a hole and covered with sand?

How can this be? They went to school. They played in the garden, they sang songs in the backseat of our car. Buried? I wanted to shout, cry, scream, but the drugs kept me trapped.

"In Durban," I said abruptly, in my zombie-like state.

Ruby took over. "Adam is in no condition to go to Durban," she said as quietly and soothingly as she could. "It is best for them to be buried in Balfour."

I nodded and agreed wordlessly. Then came the next question – the venue of the funeral. I held Adam's eldest brother in high esteem. I mechanically mentioned his name.

We left the hospital, Adam by ambulance, I with Adam's brother in his car, with my sister Fazila who had arrived from Durban. The journey appeared long and interminable. When we reached the house, we were confronted by a huge crowd, pressed into the courtyard and overflowing from the rooms which had been emptied of all furniture, the floors covered with blankets. As I was conducted into the main room, I heard my father say, "We have become beggars. The children were our wealth."

I entered the room and a stillness descended as all eyes turned on me, in sympathy and in curiosity. How did a mother grieve when rendered childless in one stroke! My eyes fell on the three bodies on the floor, wrapped in their white cotton shrouds, heads turned to one side. People moved to make space for me besides my daughters. Adam was brought in on his stretcher. My niece Soomaya, lifted the shroud to reveal their faces. I gazed on them, my eyes travelling from one to the other, back and forth. Pretty faces, looking like angels, pretty as ever, like angels always are. At that moment I could not believe this was happening. It all seemed like a nightmare. I became totally numb. I stared at the people around the room, praying and hoping that someone would slap me and tell me this is all a dream and my girls would wake up soon and life will be "normal" again. However, deep inside me I knew that that was not going to happen. I was quiet and in control, or possibly the drugs were in control. The tears streamed down my face.

I looked at Adam and the tears were streaming down his face too, and he made a gesture that signified resignation and patience. The room filled with murmurs of the word most commonly offered in consolation.

"*Sabr*! *Sabr*!" (Patience)

ADAM: I remember the next day. That was the day the ambulance came to transport me to Balfour and I was told that one of my daughters had passed away. But somehow, and I can't up to today work out how, I felt we had lost all three of them. It was just a feeling that I had in my gut, a feeling that we had lost all three. Noorjehan was in the car in the front and I had two of my friends, Danny and Dee, sitting with me in the ambulance that was taking me to Balfour.

Heading for Balfour was the most painful journey I had ever undertaken. In spite of being in an ambulance, I was smoking incessantly, trying to distract myself and hoping that I would never reach there. And, somewhere deep within myself, there was hope – hope, the mother of all men. It was the hope that I hadn't lost ALL my children.

But all journeys eventually come to an end. We finally reached Balfour and I was taken into the room where my beloved daughters were, ready for the final rites. There they were, my three girls: my world, my future, my dream. Gone now, forever.

All I wanted to do was hug them, plant a tiny kiss on their foreheads, caress their cheeks with my fingers. But it was not to be, it is forbidden to us to make any overt displays of emotion. So there I was, paralyzed with shock and a thousand other sensations, my brain refusing to process the reality.

And, because I was on a stretcher, it was decided that I could not go to the graveyard. As a result, I lost out on that final goodbye and the sense of closure.

I was not sure how Noorjehan was coping, because on the very same day I was transported by ambulance to Johannesburg Hospital – the accident had fractured my lumbar vertebrae, and there was a distinct possibility that I would not walk again. In my grief, I could not come to terms with this impending danger.

ॐ

NOORJEHAN: I wanted to be alone with my children, to embrace them, kiss them, hold them in my arms. Such demonstrations were not allowed. I didn't want to make them in public. I wanted private time, private space, but the funeral moved according to prescribed ritual.

"Oh Shamima! Oh Humeira! Oh Nadia!" I called wordlessly in my heart, the decorum instilled in me keeping me enslaved from crying out, to release some of my pent up emotion and pain.

I wanted to mummify them so that I could keep them with me forever. Finally, the rituals were read and I knew the time was close to them being taken away. I had always taught my girls to be dignified and to be ladies and I wanted to act like a lady, for them.

The time arrived for the bodies to be taken; the men came in, men of the family, and lifted my children. I could do nothing to restrain them. The *fateha* was said and my daughters were gone.

To this day I am overcome with regret and remorse as I feel that I had never said a proper goodbye. I hadn't held them in my arms. I didn't cry my tears over their faces. I was told that, according to our religion, to have done that would have been to cause them unimaginable pain, to burden them with sin, my sin of excessive grief. Once the bodies are bathed, under Islamic law, we are not allowed to touch them.

They took Shamima first and stretched her out on the floor in her funeral shroud. I wanted to grab the man's shirt or hands and hold him back. They then lifted Humeira and lastly Nadia and they were taken away to the hearses. My children were gone forever.

The spaces that they had occupied on the floor were empty. I felt that they were sacred spaces. I wanted them to be left untouched, but they were occupied almost instantly by the women who had stood up to allow the men to take the bodies for burial. I wanted to follow the men and to follow the vehicles bearing my children, but years of breeding restrained me and I sank into my space on the floor, helpless.

Women relatives began clearing the floor, spreading white paper on the blankets and bringing in the food which they began serving. People came by to commiserate, endless rows of people kissing me, embracing me, comforting me. I remained numb and unresponsive. Ruby was urging me to eat, I turned my face away. It was turning out to be a normal day for the others. The room filled with their presence as they greeted each other, chatted and smiled and enjoyed the food.

That evening, before departing for Middelburg, my parents' home, I visited my daughters' graves. My mother had made me promise that I would behave with decorum, that I would not break down. I controlled myself at the grave site, but I was overcome with the urge to remove the freshly shovelled soil from the mounds that covered their bodies. I had the strong urge to remove my daughters and carry them away in my arms to some place, somewhere safe and warm, where no one could interfere, restrain and read me the strictures about what was allowed and what was forbidden. I wanted so much to talk to them, to tell them that it was **their** obligation to bury us and not ours to bury them. I had never allowed my girls to attend funerals. I had protected them from such sadness; now they had become funerals in themselves. I faced fate wordlessly, neither complaining nor questioning. This unbearable loss was the meaning of our marriage, Adam's and mine. Fate had brought us together to stand up to this test. We would have to live with it.

We departed for Middelburg from the graveyard. The journey was made in total silence. My mother had decided that that was where I should be. My mother and sister gave me all the support they could. I had not eaten or drunk anything for over thirty hours. They saw to it that I took my meals. My mother slept beside me and consoled me each time my sleep was interrupted by bouts of sobbing. The dawn Azaan stirred me and I woke in a burst of tears, screaming and shouting and calling out to my daughters. My father was at my side intoning, "*Sabr, Sabr.*" I screamed. I did not know what *sabr* was. All I knew was that I wanted my daughters, not *sabr.*

What was the point of wanting what you can no longer have, my mother counselled, but I was way beyond counselling.

Sixteen

ADAM: Whilst I was in hospital, friends and family visited me regularly. I have very little recollection of that time. I felt as if a fog had descended over me and I had no awareness of time and space.

I was in hospital for quite some time.

Noorjehan came over every day and she pretended that she was okay, but I could see that she was not okay, she had broken a lot of ribs. And she was coping, in her usual spartan way, with the loss of our daughters.

Nothing prepares us to deal with the pain of losing a loved one. We go religiously to our temples, churches, synagogues and mosques, and we learn the efficacy of prayer, but not how to cope with grief. When death comes, it rides in on a dark horse. It strikes us squarely in the face, it wrenches our heart apart, and then leaves us bereft and, strangely, in denial.

Here I was, in hospital. People came, whispered words of condolence, and moved on. Occasionally, someone would bring his daughter with him, in the belief that I would, somehow, obtain comfort from that. Of course, it was the height of stupidity and only added to my pain.

Noorjehan visited me daily, without fail. We didn't talk much, we were beyond words. She sat like a robot, pecked me on the cheek and, after a while, she left. Like the living dead, and so was I. Nothing was fun anymore, not even food. I love food normally but it had now become tasteless, like sawdust.

That was when Noorjehan and I were forced to make a supreme decision: we had to find a way to put it all behind us. Not to forget, because that was impossible and neither of us believed in kidding ourselves. But we had to move forward, we still had each other and that became our greatest comfort, something we could build a future on.

ૐ

NOORJEHAN: The first three days of March had been consumed by the accident and the funeral. On the fourth day my mother took me to her home in Middelburg whilst Adam had returned to the hospital in Johannesburg to be operated on. I telephoned Adam at the hospital and spoke to him and on the fifth day made my first visit, thereafter visiting him daily, making the two hour journey to and from Middelburg. This went on for four weeks but I found it therapeutic as it helped me to keep my mind off the children.

But tongues were wagging. The gossips claimed that I should be staying with Adam at the hospital. Everyone had an opinion and was making decisions for me, not listening to what I, or my body needed. Adam finally put his foot down. He did not want me to stay with him out of concern for my comfort. As he said, there was too much disturbance at night. But the reality was that a temporary coldness had set in between us. It would pass but not before it became evident to others and they took a hand in trying to eliminate it.

Every day, on returning from hospital, everybody was telling me what was good or bad for me. People came to sympathise. Some wanted to know what happened but I was too exhausted to keep repeating the same story and sometimes I just looked at them and sometimes I just cried.

Some people said, "You shouldn't be alone in the bedroom;" others said, "Leave her alone, she needs to be alone;" and yet others said, "It's not good for her to be alone." Again, everyone was trying to control me. No one was listening to me and how I felt or what I really needed.

The pain of loss and my husband being hurt overtook the physical pain from my cracked ribs and the stitches in my hands and on my face. The mental pain completely overshadowed the physical.

Adam had changed tremendously. He was, and is, a gentleman through and through. He was one of those people who thought he was invincible and nothing would ever touch him in his life. Things always went well for him. He achieved what he wanted to achieve. He became the first doctor in the family. To him he owed a lot to his family by becoming the first professional man, thinking that others in succeeding generations would follow his example.

Adam remained in hospital all of four weeks. He couldn't walk normally and had to have a lot of physiotheraphy. There was a time when the doctors gave up on his arm and I worried that he wouldn't be able to resume his dental practice. But, through the grace of Allah, and his tremendous self-will, he recovered in all respects.

Unbearable recriminations replaced my unbearable grief. I recoiled in horror from myself. They used to say of widows that they were witches who had eaten up their husbands. How did one describe a mother who had killed her children? How could I escape myself? Where could I go? I could not go to their father or their uncles, or aunts, or grandparents. In that state, I went into a stupor and have no doubt I became a terrible burden to everyone around.

When I came out of the stupor as I did, periodically and mercifully, I was depressed and useless. When I think back on that time, I am surprised that I am alive today. What kept me alive? I believe that despite everything, there was somewhere within me a faith in myself, in my capacity to keep my babies safe. The accident had not been due to my neglect. It hadn't been due to an error in my driving. I had tried to keep the car on the road and in control. The problem was not with me. It was with the car. Something had gone wrong with the accelerator. I wanted the car tested from bumper to bumper, inside out. It is so easy to dismiss a woman driver. My brother insisted I drop it. What did it matter? The accident had happened. How and why was pointless. But I continued to insist on a thorough assessment of the car. I wanted to prove that there was something wrong with the car. I wanted professional advice. I wasn't content with conjectures. Those around me didn't believe there **was** something wrong with the car. That frustrated me. I was overpowered by them and overruled. I was left with the burden of blame. If there was nothing wrong with the car, then I alone was to blame. Nobody understood my great need to exonerate myself. All my efforts to clear my name were in vain. My life was taken over by others. I was a woman. Women were bad drivers. That was the general verdict and I couldn't live with it. Newspapers now say that women drivers are safer than men.

ঽ

ADAM: When our daughters died it was as if part of us had died, it was the most disorienting period in our lives. When a child dies our future expectations and dreams pass on with them. But we were mature enough to discontinue playing the blame game. We learned to accept that some things are beyond our control, that we were not in total command of our destiny. What was meant to be, would be.

ঽ

NOORJEHAN: I didn't know it at the time but I had more grief coming my way.

The condolences were just thinning out when I had a visit from the police. I listened in shock, not quite comprehending the inspector who said they had come to question me about the accident; they were investigating a charge of culpable homicide against me. "Culpable homicide?" I queried, "What is that?" Adam was in the hospital at the time. I turned to my brother for an explanation. He avoided my eyes and looked away. The inspector explained in his heavy Afrikaans accent. He said it straight, pulling no punches and wasting no extraneous words on my sensitivities. He had definitely not come to sympathise; he wanted to charge me for murdering my children!

Up to now, I had been too buried in my grief to realise that there was another side to the tragedy that had struck us. We hadn't just lost our children. I was deemed to have killed them. I was now overcome with the horror of it.

I was the driver of the car and my children were dead. Who knew that better than I?

I was suddenly overcome with a desire to be punished, as harshly as possible. Whilst my brother concentrated on having the charges dropped, I wanted to be jailed. I wanted to be tried. I wanted to be sentenced. And yet there was another side of me that revolted at the idea that I be charged with killing my children, who were more to me than life itself. What mother, what kind of mother would kill her own children? I asked this question of myself over and over again and fantasised putting it to the judge in court.

Up to this time I had experienced only kindness and concern from my friends and relatives. Now, all of a sudden, I felt them retreat from me in horror. Is this all it takes, I wondered, to create a rift in a lifetime of friendship? I couldn't help concluding that I could do without such false relationships.

Thank God there was no other car involved so there were no other burdens to carry otherwise it would have been too much for me to bear.

Forty days passed and the official period of mourning ended with the last of the Thursday fatehas and the dinner that followed. The traffic of comforters waned and stopped.

Seventeen

NOORJEHAN: We flew to Durban with my parents, Adam's elder brother and his wife. Nobody knew we were coming except my friend Vassie. Adam's brother had booked first class and, because of Adam's back, we got on and off the plane on a hoist.

I cried the whole time during the one hour flight. I didn't want to return home. How would I deal with the sight of their rooms? The table setting for five people that would now only be for two? How could I go into their bedrooms, the bathroom, through their clothing and school things?

They passed away on March 2nd ... on March 3rd they were buried and gone. The Sunday never happened.

I thought of the day we had left Durban, a family of five. Now only the two of us remained, and an empty house.

Adam and I broke down and I don't know whether we would have coped at all if my parents and his brother and sister-in-law had not been there to support us.

I looked for Humeira's drawings that she had stuck on the TV cabinet. They were not there. I looked around for them, frantically, and never found them.

I looked for Nadia's play-dough, with her imprints, that she used to make rotis in her toy utensils while I did the real cooking, but I could not find that either. The pens that Humeira had used to draw with ... gone. Someone had hidden away things that they thought would provoke painful memories.

I screamed like a mad woman. I opened all the cupboards. I expected to feel at home but it didn't feel like home, it felt like my privacy had been invaded. They took away the only grief I could anchor to. I had nothing to hold my grief to, everything was violated. The only place that belonged to the five of us was stripped from us. It wasn't my home. I had lost my anchor.

I eventually went to the bedrooms and I went through the children's clothes, touching them, smelling them, kissing them. How long would the smell last? How long would I continue, lost in relics? I kissed their shoes, I looked for hair. There was hair and brushes and toothpaste left there. I didn't want anyone to go there, to touch anything. I started to treat the rooms like a shrine, which I know now was wrong. I had nowhere I could close myself off.

I looked around the dinner table, three familiar faces – adorable, beautiful faces were missing. Shamima, Humeira and Nadia's chairs were empty. I was angry and my anger took over. I began kicking Nadia's feeding chair. What right had it to stand there in silence as if awaiting Nadia, when she would never return to her seat?

Adam restrained me. "Don't destroy the chair. Leave it. It's Nadia's."

And that was when I heard someone shout, I swear I heard it clearly: "Daddy has come home. Run! Run! Humsie hide," Shamima's voice rang out in excitement. Nadia was joining her sisters on unsteady feet. Were they under the chair, behind the curtain? Where? Where? Then it hit me – they were not there. The children's voices were coming out of my mind. Humsie was not holding her breath in expectation of being caught. I broke down and sobbed uncontrollably.

I cried and cried when I realised that there were no little feet running around helter skelter. No laughter held in their little chests in expectation of being caught at any moment. None of their laughter flooding the room in merry, excited squeals. Absolute nothingness, just the painful sounds of silence.

My mind started racing and questions kept flooding through it. How would I face Eid, with no little hands to be spread with henna, no happy arms taking trays of sweetmeats to the neighbours and returning with gifts of silver coins; for Humsie that's all that Eid was about, the Eidie? Now there were no little girls to dress prettily.

At Diwali, the girls had followed our neighbours and put out little diyas in rows all around our verandah, and at Easter I had hid Easter eggs and they had played games finding them.

The memories came flooding back fast and furious.

We had looked forward to Saturdays and Sundays – they were family days, picnic days. Now they were empty, pointless days – no children tugging at my apron, "Mummy it is getting late, let's go." No one urging me to let go of the cooking and the chores, no packing into the car, singing songs on our way to the North Coast or the South Coast, where the waves rolled on the sand; no drives to the burger stand in the evenings, no trips to the ice cream parlor, no little people spending weekends with my daughters.

I wanted to put the clock back; go back to the days, the weeks, the months before the accident. I wanted my children so desperately, I went back in time and began living in the time in which my children lived. It was all so surreal. Time was the only reality and I played with time, not as it was, but as it had been, filled with laughter and the tears of my children.

My mind kept reverting to the past. Our lives had been so complete – a beautiful home, a very comfortable income and three adorable daughters admired by all. Had we grown conceited? Inflated with pride? Had our bubble been burst as a warning? Anything, anything, but not this. Allah took and Allah gave. Allah was so powerful and so merciful. Perhaps He would give us again, the same daughters, my Shamima, Humeira and Nadia. Adam wanted us to start again. I froze at the very thought of it. I didn't want other children. I wanted our children, those that we had lost, returned to me and us. The thought of adoption played in Adam's mind, but he dared not raise it with me. He understood my frailty.

In our hopelessness and helplessness, we began blaming each other in unbroken silence. I harboured dark thoughts against Adam and they remained bottled within me. I was thinking and yet I couldn't think. I was brain dead. The doctor saw both of us. He did the usual thing; he gave us both tranquilizers, but our pain was too deep, even the tranquilizers couldn't reach it.

We were not communicating with each other. I suffered withdrawal symptoms. I stopped talking with him. I was dead within myself. Neither Adam nor I were in a condition to console and support each other. I was a zombie. We coped with drugs, without them I was and felt desperate.

The fact that I was in the driving seat haunted me continuously. I blamed Adam for imposing the driving on me while he reclined his seat and slept.

I had the terrible feeling that he blamed the accident on my driving, and he was cursing himself for entrusting the driving to me. It is customary that the wife was generally treated as a minor, patronised and rarely given serious responsibility. I had taken pride in Adam's faith in me. I was his chief aid in his surgery. He left the buying and planning to me and consulted me in practically every move he made. Now I resented that he had entrusted me with the driving.

Then I blamed him for leaving me to drive a car that was faulty. After all it had broken down in Ladysmith. What sort of repair job had been done on it? He had been in charge. I had nothing to do with the repairs. He had insisted on us driving to Balfour in a car that we would and could not be sure of; now I was to be blamed for the accident. If I harboured blame against him, how much more blame did he harbour against me? At the end of the day, all said and done, I had been driving the car.

Adam and I needed to reach out to each other as never before, but we found that we could not. While we shared a terrible tragedy, we had plunged into an unbearable mourning. We had come to the point where we were near strangers. We had not grown with each other; we could not respond as one nor could we comfort each other as one. We were apart and the loss of our daughters could not, and did not, bring us together. Instead it manifested itself in my sudden frigidity. I could not respond to Adam's touch. I recoiled from him. I did not know what it did to him, I was too absorbed in my own feelings. It was as if our sorrow was not mutual, as if we did not share the same tragedy.

Our friends and relatives saw our apartness, saw that we did not talk to each other any more and we avoided each other, and they became very worried. I was kept on tranquilisers and this deepened my zombie-like state. Adam was not in the same anaestheised condition. He was in control of himself although he had suffered the same loss as I had. We became the objects of concerned attention and discussion and someone then had the bizarre idea of putting us together in a hospital ward for a day and night in an attempt to get us to communicate with each other. It didn't work. We spent the night staring at the ceiling and we were both extremely relieved when daylight broke and we said our prayers. That was our only mutuality.

The coldness between us did not end for months, though it mellowed a little. The presence of Adam's nephews who came to live with us whilst they attended university helped. They provided us with an intermediary channel to reach out to one another in our grief. Without them those first few months after the funeral would have been altogether unbearable.

The days passed on; our grief did not. It continued weighing heavily on our hearts. We could not face each other. We could not talk to one another. It was as if our only bond was through our children and now, with them gone, the bond too was gone, or so we thought at the time. We blamed ourselves and we blamed each other for precautions we had not taken, for omissions and for commissions.

My mother stayed on for three weeks before my father came to fetch her. I cried and clung to her. I didn't want her to go. I couldn't make it without her. I couldn't cook. No! No! No! I could do nothing without her. She said she would return at Eid. I dreaded Eid. It was the children's day, they would be up very early, anxious not to miss a minute of the day, prancing about in their fineries, waiting at the door for Adam to return from mosque and sit at the table to be served Eid milk and samoosas.

Adam was not allowed to bend for three months after his operation. I helped him put his clothes on after his shower and tried to do more for him which, being as independent as he is, he would not allow. He was an excellent patient, demanding little, never showing any sign of irritation.

Eighteen

ADAM: On our return to Durban, we walked into this very empty house. We had lots of friends at the house. But it was, to us, totally desolate. It was dead, it was like walking into a mortuary, into a funeral parlour. The joy that was there had gone.

I began to look for signs of them, for some memorabilia, to see if anything was left of them. We had to, for the sake of our sanity, discontinue doing that. And the table, as Noorjehan couldn't help noticing, was empty.

Friends came with their children. I became envious of them and I thought, "Where are my children? Why are they not with me?"

I had some religious people and they came over and mouthed the usual nonsense: I should count myself lucky, my three daughters would keep the doors to heaven open and I would go through them gloriously. I know they meant well, but their puerile stories made me angry.

It made no sense to me at the time. It still doesn't make sense.

Noorjehan and I, under one roof, became like two ships passing in the night. She was much angrier than I was. She wanted to somehow get out of my life. I was fine in the sense that I still loved her very much, I'm sure she loved me too but her anger was getting in the way.

Noorjehan tried to introduce an element of routine in our lives. For a while it worked. And, of course, we were fortunate in that we had some good friends. Noorjehan was very close to Vasie, who was a school teacher. She was South Indian and was married to a Muslim teacher. They didn't have any children of their own so they had doted on our children. It was good having them around. Their grief was quite as intense as ours but they were a good support group for us. We could cry with them and we could laugh with them. They came home frequently, and it was good for Noorjehan as well, becaue they helped with the cooking and cleaning and kept our spirits up.

And so they provided an anchor in our lives, both Vasie and Hussein. They would literally be there twenty-four hours a day and it was good for both Noorjehan and I. Vasie, particularly, was the soul of humanity and she unobtrusively led Noorjehan out of her grief or at least to cope with it.

At the time, I had eleven surgeries, about six doctors working for me, six dentists and, after my brother and in-laws went away, Noorjehan took me to the surgeries to check that everything was working smoothly.

A few of the dentists were related to me, and I would have thought it's the non-family dentists who would be a problem. As it turned out, those who were related to me became my worst enemies. They began to literally blackmail me into transferring the surgery to them. They knew that I was going to be out of action for the next six months, at the least.

They were aware that I was vulnerable and were holding a gun to my head. I never realised that you could get people like these in your life. But tragedy teaches you a lot about human behaviour and how opportunistic people become.

Noorjehan was concerned about our finances. I didn't know what was happening at my surgeries and I didn't really care at the time. If I could have helped it I would have thrown it all up. I told Noorjehan that I needed to sell everything and just get out of it and not do anything, just be like a hobo on the streets.

Noorjehan would have none of that, we were very young and we had a long life to look forward to. Throwing in the towel was stupid.

After about a year, as my back started feeling better, Noorjehan assisted me out of the bath, because I couldn't bend down. She would wipe my feet, dry me and help me with my trousers. That was good because it gave us something to do, we were occupied with each other and Noorjehan had somebody to care for like a baby.

She drove me to the surgery and I started checking the books and I found that we were not doing very well. Everybody was taking advantage of the situation. Gradually, I got to the stage where I needed to sell one or two of the surgeries and lighten the load that I had. I could not carry on like this much longer.

We had a few very good friends. We had Danny and Dee, Vasie and one or two others but somehow I found it very difficult to socialise.

I kept thinking of my own children each time I looked at theirs. I felt that my children would have been about their age and they would have been laughing, dressing up funnily, doing whatever children that age do. So, whilst I started withdrawing from my friends, Noorjehan encouraged the children to come to our place because they were our daughters' friends. I simply wanted to withdraw from society and live a hermit-like existence.

Noorjehan would have our friends over for dinner, or simply for sandwiches. At the time I didn't appreciate what I viewed as an intrusion into my grief, and I reacted to her efforts with anger. I failed to see that she was indulging in a form of therapy, for both of us.

Noorjehan became my saviour and my guide. Although we had our problems, mostly emanating from the accident, she advised me when I was busy selling the surgeries and one or two little properties I owned. She said it was not the right time for me to do these things because I was not thinking clearly and I should postpone all my decisions until I returned to some sort of stability.

She was right, of course. In the depths of my grief I was not behaving rationally.

There were good friends around me, well-meaning friends who did their best to help me cope, but I was beyond reason. In my pain I had become somewhat self-centred – how could they possibly understand the magnitude of the tragedy, without having experienced the anguish of the loss?

Noorjehan became my refuge, she moored me to the real world and saved me from myself.

Nineteen

NOORJEHAN: It has been said that the barrier between those who live and those who pass on is impenetrable, yet I believe the sheer will of those separated is so strong that communications occur in some form or other. These communications are in themselves evidence of the life beyond. There has to be life after death. There is no evidence that there isn't, except the opinion of skeptics. I cannot accept such opinions. There is too much at stake for me to crush myself with such negativity.

But where does one begin, who could guide us on such a journey? This was not like visiting a foreign country. We were contemplating a trip to the netherworld, in search of our children. This was unheard of and there were warnings against us doing so: it was against the teachings of Islam, the dead should be left in peace, God's will had been served.

Both Adam and I refused to accept it. Surely there was more to life than living simply to die. The miracle of Creation must have been conceived with a definite purpose. Our girls were out there, somewhere. It was up to us to find them.

The more we searched, the more we were told, repeatedly, that our daughters were not in this, that they were in another world safe with God where he reigned with His Angels over the entire Universe. This was a familiar Islamic picture. We knew it. We were impelled to believe it. But I wanted something more, something tangible. I became desperate. I began praying as I had never done before. The five times *namaaz* were not sufficient for me. I never left my prayer mat until I had wrung out God with my grief.

"Give me a vision of my daughters, dear God. You are all powerful, all knowing. Let them come to me in my dreams. Please let me know that they are happy with you. Is it too much to ask?"

My entreaties were met with Divine Silence.

Then I heard about people who could make contact with the dead. Could I pursue this course of action? I knew it was un-Islamic. The teaching was to leave those things to Allah. He knows best. My duty was to accept that He in his wisdom had taken my children from me. After all, it was He who had given them to me in the first place. They belonged to Him. He had taken what was His. They had been on loan to Adam and me. I heard this over and over again. I had no arguments against it. Yet I hankered after my children and if there were people who offered me an alternative I had to know about them.

"You can know, you should know, you must know." I was like a stuck record, telling myself, "I will know, I will know!"

I raised my hands to Allah, "Help me to know. You are all knowledgeable. You are pure knowledge. Give me knowledge of my children. You are all merciful. You cannot begrudge me a vision of them, or even a meeting with them."

I shuddered at these thoughts. I knew I was on dangerous ground, but I could not stop, such was my desperation, such was my need to know.

It was in this fraught state that the silence that had divided Adam and I since the accident broke. If I needed to know about my children, so did he. Eve-like, I drew him into my desire to search for our children.

My mum's friend told her about a book called *MIKE*. Initially, I was upset – the ignorant part of me. I asked my brother to get the book for me as I was not allowed by the immediate family to get such books. We couldn't find it in Durban. I phoned Mum for her friend's telephone number and she said, "Don't worry, I'll send the book to you. Just pick it up at the airport."

All I wanted was to know where my children were. In what form, I knew not. This book, I was told, would explain everything to us. Adam too became interested in the book. It gave us hope, and we were vulnerable to clinging on to the flimsiest hope.

When I read the book I was overjoyed. It changed my life and thinking. It gave me hope, and a feeling that perhaps there were some definite answers.

I gave it to Adam to read. Then we went in search of the writer.

All we had was a vague address in Pietermaritzburg. Adam and I went in search of the place. We could not find it but, on turning a corner, we saw a policeman. I asked Adam to go over and speak to him, and see if he could help us.

When Adam asked him if he could help us find anyone related to the book *MIKE*, he knew exactly who we needed to speak to as he had known the writer and had actually been a pall bearer at his funeral. He said that we needed to speak to Nine Merrington but that she was no longer in Pietermaritzburg and had moved to Sezela on the KwaZulu-Natal South Coast.

We went to Sezela to look for Nine Merrington, with no success.

By then someone had given me another book, *Voices in My Ear* by Doris Stokes. I tracked her to a number in London. The man who answered, O'Leary, invited us to a public demonstration. I said I wanted a private sitting, and he agreed to set it up for us.

We left for London with Adam's nephew, Shiraaz. He had never been abroad. We confided the purpose of our trip to no one. I told my mother we needed a change and that Adam's friends in London had offered him the use of their home while they were on holiday, and we were taking the opportunity.

We arrived in London during the first week in August. I remember this quite well because it was Shamima's birthday. August signifies a great deal for us. Shamima's birthday was on the third, Adam's on the fourth, and mine on the seventh. I kept telling myself that the time could not be merely co-incidental. God was working with us. We contacted Laurie O'Leary on our arrival in London and he gave us directions to his office.

London is cold in August, which turns its back on spring and the days are much too short. It was dark and dismal when we reached O'Leary's office. He, by contrast, was warm and welcoming.

He drove us in his car to the home of Doris Stokes, the medium whom we hoped would connect us to our children.

Doris was friendly, and asked for the names of all the members of our family, alive and deceased. Doris happened to have problems pronouncing the names. She said that troubled her, and she could promise us nothing. I assured her that we had come with an open mind.

For a while, nothing happened. We sat with our hands in our laps. And then, as we looked at her, Doris went into a trance. And then she started to speak. Her eyes had closed and her voice appeared to be coming from a distance, almost as if someone else was now talking.

"The children are singing 'Happy Birthday'."

I saw Adam start. It had been his birthday the day before.

"The eldest girl, Shamima, is caring for her younger sisters. Shamima is speaking. She says, 'Daddy you have a nasty thought in your mind. It makes me very unhappy. Don't do it.'"

We were shaken! Just before we had left for London, Adam had confided to me that he could not go on living. If we could not be a family in life, we could be one in death. We had discussed gassing ourselves in our car.

Doris went on to say that the children were in a beautiful place, and that they were very happy. Fantasy or fact, it consoled us.

Doris described the accident and the funeral and I was startled by the accuracy of her portrayal of the event. She said, "I smell no smoke, there is no fire. Just death, peaceful, painless."

I was impressed. But I am, by my very nature, a suspicious person. I needed something more, some kind of confirmation that Doris was not leading us on.

I decided to test her, and asked her to describe our home. She said there was a red settee in our living room, which I had sent away for upholstering. That was certainly true. She also told me other things about my family, things that only we knew, some of which I had forgotten. I now had no reason to doubt that she did indeed have supra-sensory perceptions.

Our first session with Doris was short. It lasted about half an hour. The second session lasted all of two hours. I had read that people who are clairvoyant find it difficult to go on beyond two hours; they find it tiring. I respected that.

A week passed and it was Bakri Eid. I phoned Laurie again and confided that I was feeling extremely low and would like to see

Doris again. I knew our chances of seeing her were slim, but, to our surprise, she agreed to see us.

I wasn't sure what I wanted, but deep inside I knew that I wanted the impossible, to turn the clock back and be with my children. She did not relieve us of our grief. It was up to us to do that.

Doris had helped our emotional state. She had convinced us that our children were with God, secure and happier than they would have been if still in our trust. We had been good parents and the children had enjoyed their interlude with us, but if we grieved, it was for ourselves, not for them. The children lived in another realm, one beyond ours, accessible to us only after death.

Doris connected us to our children emotionally, not physically. We never saw them either in vision or in voice, all communication during the seances was through her, though later, much later, I was blessed with visions. But basically during this time she was our medium. We found ourselves drawn into another world. It was an inexplicable experience, one of sheer feeling. Doris warned us that the feeling would not remain with us. We would have to develop our own sense of communication and it would come with faith in life beyond the present. She told us that religion – all religions – help, because they give us this other dimension. Our initial knowledge of that dimension is rooted in religion.

"If you do not believe in God and an afterlife," she warned, "then I am afraid I cannot help you, nor can you help yourself."

By now, we were becoming somewhat reconciled to our loss. Being away from home, finding a new source of comfort, had helped to make us more settled in our minds. We had probably needed to get away from relatives and friends who, having grieved with us, re-lived that grief with us, entrenching it. We needed to be free of that. And the trip had served that purpose. We were beginning to gain a new insight into people, and picking up on some of the selfish streak that they began to display towards us. We returned refreshed, but now faced the reproach of our relatives. How could we, still in mourning, have just taken off without a word to them? Somehow they all felt that we had let them down. That, of course, had never been our intention.

We had enlargements made of the best photographs we had of our children. We hung them prominently on the wall of our house. Amazingly, some of our relatives were appalled. They said it was un-Islamic to have photographs, and even more so of the deceased. I didn't argue with them. I wanted to keep their images alive. They were my children, my memories were still filled with them.

Only those who had lost a loved one could understand that. And we had lost three of our beloved children. There was no way that we would allow parochial and narrow-minded individuals to dictate to us.

The gossips, with nothing to keep themselves occupied, were now out in full force, they accused me of whatever their sick minds could conjure, including that I was now a Christian. All this simply because of a few photographs. "Where," I quietly asked, "does it say in the Quran that you cannot have photographs?"

And, as if I was not in enough pain already, the vicious rumour began to circulate that I had lost my children because I was very modern in my outlook and that God had punished me.

Were these people those who truly believe in God? Did they not know that gossip is a cardinal sin in Islam?

I remain linked to death, dreading funerals, but wanting to reach out to the bereaved, particularly when the bereavement was the result of an accidental death. I had, and still have, a compulsive desire to talk to them, to relate my own loss in the hope that it will offer some comfort to the newly bereaved, that they are not alone, and that I share their tragedy.

Twenty

NOORJEHAN: We travelled a lot. Twice a year we would go abroad, often attending Adam's conferences. We met a lot of people and invariably the talk turned to family and children.

"How many children do you have? How old are they?" they would ask me. I told them, "I don't know if you want to hear my story," but, after a little prompting, I told it all the same and I saw the shock and stunned looks on their faces, and then the curiosity finally got to them and they would ask, "How do you survive?", "How do you remain sane?"

How do we survive? Wisdom has taught me there are two kinds of problems in life, God-given and Man-made. There is nothing you can do about God-given problems. One has to accept them. I rationalise to myself that God puts calamities and tragedies in the path of those he loves most. That thought is what keeps me ticking and alive.

We went for *Umrah* to be nearer God. We were comforted, circumnambulating the *Ka'bah*, praying in the *Harem Sharif* in Mecca and in Medina. We returned calmer within ourselves, though our grief remained intact. Each time we returned from somewhere, the criticisms started. This particular time it was that I hadn't adopted the complete *hijab* on my return. I had decided I had more serious things to do, than an outward show of piety.

At the time of writing this, it has been thirteen years since the time of the accident, but every year when the day comes it strikes me again with the same pain as on that first day when within a matter of minutes we lost all our three daughters. I shudder at the thought of it. This pain is with me all the time. However, I do not wish to be without it, as for me in this moment not to have that pain would be to be without my daughters. It is all I have of them

– the memory of their short lives, and the ache of that brutal loss. My pain is now grooved into my being like a chronic disease; I cope with it as I cope with myself, and with each passing year on this day it flares up, acute and uncontrollable as on the day I first became afflicted with it.

Adam, I felt, was far more composed than I. I put it down to men grieving differently. Adam, I felt, had put everything in a closet and shut the doors. Sometimes I can relate to the pain and his outward appearance of a lack of emotion. There is not a day when he leaves the house without reciting the Fatiha for his daughters.

ૐ

NOORJEHAN: Sometimes when I cannot sleep, I look at the photographs and cannot believe that we had three children and now we have none. Humsie told me not very long before she left us, "Mummy, do not buy me any more clothes, I have got lots of clothes."

I found that rather strange at the time but realised that she was one of those children who was not interested in clothes. She was caught up with the marvel of nature. She used to sprout her own beans, with cotton wool and water, and was fascinated when they germinated.

All these memories make me wonder what they would have looked like today had they lived, what sort of in-laws we would have had, and, most importantly, how many grandchildren would have been tumbling around us.

Pain is not something that you can run away from, even when you are travelling, you carry it with you. And it can be a form of escapism from reality. We have the responsibility of living our lives to the fullest until our time in this world is done, and we must do so. I know this to be the truth, and pray daily to Allah to give me the strength to live this truth. I was thrown into the deep end of the ocean and swimming ashore continues to be a daily battle.

Initially I found that I couldn't get myself to attend weddings. Each invitation reminded me of my niece's wedding at which Nadia was to be a flower girl. I still cannot attend funerals. I always see three corpses where there is only one.

But we cope with our tragedy and God helps and His help gives us strength to survive and continue. Our daughters continue to grow in our minds and live in our hearts.

Grief can also be very selfish, in the sense that one tends to think only of oneself. We would probably have been grandparents by now and if not, there would have been one of them who would have possibly followed in their father's footsteps. We would have had extended families via marriage and so on, but after a while one comes to realise that they chose to be here for a fixed period of time and their time on earth was done. It was then that I realised that they are in a better world. Of course, the physical longing will always be there but one does have choices. One has to complete one's own journey and go on, as painful as it may be. When looking back I reflect on the fact that they had their own souls, and that their behaviour was rather unique. I was and always will be proud of their particular mannerisms, their individualities and their uniqueness. In my own private way, I will always celebrate that reality. As for the gossips, when their time comes, they will have to account to God for their vicious behaviour.

ॐ

ADAM: Somewhere, along the way, perhaps two or three months later, I decided that we needed to see a psychiatrist. Our marriage was becoming shaky and, we were beginning to drift apart.

Neither Noorjehan nor I believed in a make-believe world. We were both far too practical for that. We accepted that, by their very nature, marriages have their good times and their lean times.

I didn't kid myself that marriages are made in heaven.

When we went to the psychiatrist, we were told he was a

Muslim psychiatrist. I'm not sure what that was supposed to mean. A pscyhiatrist, after all, is a psychiatrist, whatever his religious persuasion.

Anyway, he told us that he had many Muslim couples amongst his patients, and that it was obvious that the problem stemmed from what he called "the empty nest syndrome".

I'd often heard about an empty nest syndrome, but never understood it from the point of view of psychiatrists. He said that, normally, what tends to happen is there is no solidification of the marriage. In the first year love is the paramount emotion and it colours the entire relationship. And, before you truly get to know each other, you're already planning a family. When the kids come we are immersed in parenthood and our dreams are put on hold – the honeymoon is over before it even started. The joint responsibility of being a father and a mother take over. The male in the family is out of his depth – the time and effort required to inculcate decent values into the children is beyond him.

In the olden days it was fine. We had extended families. We had a whole village; we had relatives with whom we could share the responsibilities of caring for the children. Nowadays, we have nuclear families. We have two or three children that we hyper-parent.

We want the children to have everything of the best. We want them to excel at so many things. We want them to do ballet, to do piano, to do singing, to do soccer, to do sports and the father, in this early stage of life, is busy working to make a living. The mother is caught up with carting the kids around and becomes the general dogsbody. By the end of the day everybody is absolutely tired and the man finds that the woman is too exhausted to even have sex.

This creates problems in the early years of marriage and besides, the children are the main focus of married life. It distracts the couple from creating a lasting bond. It is only later in their lives, when the children are off their hands and they are on their own once more, that the problem of compatibility rears its ugly head.

In our case the problem was far more serious – we were

blaming each other for the tragedy and all the minor incidents during the early years of our marriage suddenly resurfaced and acquired a seriousness that hitherto had not existed. This is when the "blame game" begins and the marriage starts to slide.

Life takes on a semblance of simple existence, a façade. Outwardly we project an image of happiness, living more for society's approval rather than for ourselves.

It's an empty life, devoid of love and caring. What keeps us together is fear, the fear of treading into the unknown, the realisation that to contemplate separation is stepping into a void from which there is no turning back.

Strangely, within these terrifying contradictions, we stumble into a comfort zone. We live in separate rooms, sleep on our own, but continue to exist under one roof. Somehow it becomes a routine that provides a sense of solace, the security that somebody is there when you come home. I have seen this phenomenon often, people live like that and I am repelled by it. I appreciate that this is done to obtain society's acceptance, and not to rock the family boat. So, yes, we had come full circle really. We had gone for almost a year to psychiatrists, trying to get some assistance. One of the problems with psychiatrists is that they prescribe anti-depressants instead of talking to you and trying to be marriage counsellors. They tend to experiment with drugs and drugs have their own problems, they have their own complications, they have their own side effects. They make you lethargic, they give rise to symptoms that you've never had before. You become like a walking pharmacy, because psychiatrists test the drugs for the drug companies so you become like guinea pigs. We became, initially, like guinea pigs.

After several months, I gave up all the anti-depressants. I said they had too many negative side effects for my liking. Noorjehan had also discontinued taking them because they caused complications in her life, complications she found difficult to handle.

In the midst of all this, we were still at loggerheads; there was no resolution to our conflict. There was a little more sanity in our lives. There was a little more acceptance, perhaps only a wee bit, but the initial shock was over, we had come to terms with it and had accepted the pain of the tragedy. Now we had to live with the loss. We had to live with the emptiness in our lives.

In coping with these issues, the belief that we had no future had insidiously crept into us. Our entire life had been constructed around our children, and on our children's children. We had dreamed of a large extended family, continuing far into the distant future. Sadly, we had to accept that that dream had been exploded, that our horizon was very bleak indeed. There didn't seem to be light at the end of the tunnel. However, we carried on because we had to. We had life, and so we had to exist.

The only thing that gave me solace were the books that Noorjehan kept on buying. She bought books about near death experiences. Many such experiences were about people who had technically died on the operating table and had been brought back by medical science. They recounted some wonderful, wonderful experiences of how beautiful it was in these few minutes of death. What they experienced – the tunnel and the light, the humanity and the lovely feeling, the beautiful feeling of out of body experiences. And a lot of people talked about not wanting to return to their bodies.

So, those were very soothing to our minds. That gave us hope that there may be a beautiful place somewhere out there and that the children had gone into that serene and peaceful place. It gave us some consolation. But, being human and naturally sceptical, we had our moments of doubt and disbelief. You can read and be presented with a host of close encounters of another world, but until you see it yourself, have irrefutable proof of such a place, it remains an unacceptable mystery.

But we read many of those books. Also lots of books about psychics and, as Noorjehan explains, going to Doris Stokes was a great source of comfort to our hearts. We felt pretty good after that. Just for that moment. Just for those couple of hours, we felt 'Yes', there is some sort of relief that has come to us.

Twenty-One

ADAM: Besides psychiatrists, we needed some additional assistance. Nobody understood what was happening to us. Nobody at all. Even the psychiatrists did not understand. People always met you on the street, they always talk about how they lost their parents, how they lost their mother or their grandfather. They did not understand that losing a child or a spouse is a different experience altogether. It was done with good intentions but very annoying and at the time seemed insensitive. I was angry over the tragedy disturbing our tranquility and our future. Anger does not have to be logical or valid.

We then decided that we needed somebody and so we went to Compassionate Friends. Compassionate Friends is a group that deals with people that lose their children. We had a nice little group. It was in a church somewhere in Durban. They used to meet once or twice a month.

We initially went there and when we told our story everybody was totally shocked because most people that were at Compassionate Friends had lost a child. I remember that there was a Scottish lady and her husband that had lost a child in childbirth. It was still born. And for the next two full sessions, it was an hour, hour and a half, she took the podium and kept on telling us how difficult it had been for her. And I found this very difficult to accept and the second time she did that, we came back home and I told Noorjehan, I said, "Look, I don't really want to go to this Compassionate Friends because I think that we have lost more in terms of, you know, tragedy. We have had a bigger tragedy. And this woman keeps on carrying on, you know, telling us how big her tragedy was."

Noorjehan quite wisely told me, "That is her tragedy, we need to accept her tragedy. Doesn't matter how many children you lose or how much you lose in your life, your tragedy belongs to you, and so you have to sympathise and empathise with her for her to get through it." And then I subsequently came to find out that after about six, eight months the husband and wife had divorced.

Now that seems to be a very normal sort of thing in tragedies. We saw this all along. We attended the Compassionate Friends for six to eight months. They were very helpful. They could relate to you, at least, and that was important. They could understand your grief. They could understand your crying. They could understand your anger. The ordinary person that Noorjehan calls those that are living a normal life, or so-called normal life, doesn't understand how difficult grieving becomes and what tragedy is. They expect that, in a couple of months, you will get out of the state that you are in. I suppose it makes them much more comfortable.

We tend to take comfort when we know there are other people in the same boat. However, the comfort was not fully appreciated because people had other children and I thought that it was not fair to attend Compassionate Friends because we had lost ALL our children. Noorjehan, however, was always dragging me along and saying that I needed to listen to people, and learn how they've coped. We could bond and understand each other's pain and it also allowed us a sense of privacy and a sympathetic hearing, made us less isolated and vulnerable.

The couple that were running the course are from Durban and they had lost their son and daughter-in-law, who had been murdered. Of course, they were relating an incident that had happened fifteen years or twenty years before our own tragedy, and were explaining to us how they coped with their pain. So, yes, we tried to get all sorts of help and assistance. Surprisingly, their post-tragedy relationship seemed to be rock-solid and palpable, and one could literally feel and sense it. To us it was a good omen, a mentor and hope that the relationship could emerge after such a tragedy in such a positive way.

That did, to a certain extent, help with our marriage. There were about fifteen couples in our group, and all of them had, to a greater or lesser degree, experienced major strains in their marriage. Together with the tragedy in their lives, they now had to contend with the rigours of a shaky relationship. It was what I can only call, a double tragedy.

Noorjehan and I grieved in different ways. Women hold on to everything that is around them. She wanted their room to remain undisturbed, their clothing to be in specific places. With their physical presence gone, their material belongings were the last reminder of their existence in this world. She had decided to part with their clothing gradually, in her own time and space, when she felt more comfortable to let go. It was her way of dealing with the pain.

There are no time limits we should prescribe on parting with their possessions. Well meaning people expressed concern that she was building a shrine around their room. She was asked to give all to charity, which would shower her with God's grace. They were clueless about the emotional trauma of parting with their last vestiges of remembrance. We were the custodians of their proof of existence. Giving away their clothes was like deserting the permanency of the relationship and moving on with our lives. We couldn't do that.

Twenty-Two

ADAM: After about six to eight months, when I removed my plaster, I started selling some of my dental surgeries but didn't want to move back into dentistry. Also, we didn't want to face many people and we were upset with a lot of them who did not have the courtesy of paying their respects. Noorjehan always said they were scared and I asked, "Why should they be scared? What do they have to fear?" There was anger in me, and I stopped greeting some of our friends and she told me, "You know, you need to be in their boots to understand how difficult it may be."

I started a motor dealership out in Umhlatazana Township in Chatsworth, which went well, but Noorjehan was not too happy about it. She said, "You have a profession and you need to go back to it." I was simply trying to keep myself occupied. For her it was much more difficult, being at home with nothing constructive to occupy her mind.

It took all of two years before our marriage was on track again, and that had been a very difficult time – we missed the kids and were often miserable and lonely.

With the passage of time, we learnt to get to grips with our life together and our relationship took on a distinct improvement. We began to attend functions, did a bit of socialising and even took in an occasional dinner. It hadn't been easy but we were now a little more comfortable.

Slowly, we began to merge with society. And the many Doctors' Guilds, that often tried to outdo each other by hosting the best party, helped us immensely. In the early years, before we lost our children, we regularly frequented their parties. Now, some of our very dear friends insisted that we get back into the swing of things and, with immense reluctance, we attended a few dinner and dance events.

On one of those evenings, a group of us – four couples in all – were seated at the same table. As soon as the formalites were over, (KD) Pillay, a neighbour and a very dear friend, insisted that Noorjehan should take to the floor with him. She was very reluctant. But (KD), good friend that he was, knew that we needed to be nudged in the right direction and, after some persuasion, she joined him on the floor.

Strangely, it broke the ice in Noorjehan's heart. When they returned to our table I sensed a definite lightening of her mood. The rest of that evening passed very pleasantly and, when we headed for home, there was a smile on our faces, something that hadn't happened in ages.

In re-discovering our joy in each other's company, Noorjehan and I naively thought that all our friends, without exception, would share in our newfound happiness. That was when we learned, to our dismay, that there are always small-minded people who enjoy seeing others grieving. One such person was a doctor friend of ours who snidely began to comment that we had far too quickly overcome the loss of our daughters.

That was when I first came across the German word: *Schadenfreude*. It referred to the malicious enjoyment that some people obtain from the grief that others experience. Just knowing that there were such people in the world gave me the strength to cope.

Gradually, our marriage got much better. We started to carve out a new life for ourselves and, with some of our friends, we went ballroom dancing – that was about four, four and a half years after the tragedy.

That was sometime in 1991. It was an amazing time. We met lots and lots of new friends out there. We met Muslims, Non-Muslims, other Indians, other whites, other African people. There were close to about thirty or forty couples that were there every Friday and Saturday night, to get together and practice dancing. It was a good time. I've always found that ballroom dancing is a very elegant affair. You can dress up and step out. Somehow, we found joy in that.

As much as we enjoyed dancing, we also made many good friends. And it was a lot more fun than going to some functions, where people just sit around, six or ten to a table, doing nothing but indulging in gossip.

At the dinner and dance sessions there was absolutely no time or inclination to indulge in such harmful activities. And even less time to talk. You wanted to be on the floor, the music flowing over you, the beautiful sound raising your spirit and making your heart sing.

Of course, we didn't escape the wrath of the dinosaurs in our community who were in their element. It didn't bother us. You can be certain that whatever you do, there will always be criticism from some people, especially those who have not experienced a grief such as ours. There is no escaping those armchair critics, forever on their soapbox. We found their versions of morality amusing. In their prattling they didn't, for a moment, realise that their own behaviour – the gossiping and spitting of venom – was immoral in the extreme.

Time heals all pain and life can be good and meaningful again. It could take years, depending on the depth of the tragedy and the mindset of the sufferers. We learn more about ourselves through adversity rather than from good times.

We can deny the pain or we can let it in. What we cannot escape is the reality that it could happen to any of us. If we love, then we are always vulnerable to grief.

I live by my own standards and not by the judgement of others. I subscribe to a belief in justice, and my life is moulded by it.

We know that, eventually, we will recover, become more mature, stronger, wiser and more compassionate. And when we are able to laugh again, to feel joy and a sense of peace, then we can be sure we are on the road to recovery. That will be the time to rejoice at the fact that we have survived and learned to live.

In pursuit of a little happiness in our lives, we were hurting nobody. The selfish murmurings of these false moralists, the hypocrites, was only succeeding in poisoning their own souls. We continued leading our lives, giving charity and seeing to the indigent amongst us. Our consciences were clear.

We became quite comfortable with the life we were living. I have always been of the opinion that morals are different in different religions. Each has its own version of morality. The Prophet Mohammed was different from Jesus but both were very moral people. We also find morality is viewed differently in different countries. What is moral in one country could be considered highly immoral in another. By way of simple example, here in South Africa you do on occasion see bare-breasted African women walking around in public – and that is not considered in the least immoral. In Europe and India it would be totally immoral.

In the face of so many contradictions, we needed to carve a niche for ourselves. We decided that we were not going to be a part of society nor were we going to be against society. We decided on the middle path, to follow the little light inside ourselves, and to understand ourselves.

We had also come to the conclusion that we were not born to fulfil other people's dreams or other people's wishes, whether that be our priest, the local politician, our parents or the extended families. We decided that by pandering to the desire of others we would end up missing out on our own lives. It took a lot for us to come to that realisation. It took a horrific tragedy to learn that lesson.

Prior to the tragedy, we were quite comfortable living an ordinary physical existence where you had food, drink, and physical necessities. There was no introspection in our life. We didn't need introspection. We didn't have to look into ourselves. We didn't have to find the other God. We were taught that there is a God and that's fine, let's live by what we have been taught. But then a tragedy strikes you and you need to find out and know who you are, where you come from; and you need to understand life and you seek life, you seek answers. You seek the meaning of life, your purpose in life. Were we the guide for other people to take strength from our tragedy?

Noorjehan then decided to devote a lot of her time to charitable work. The first thing she felt we needed to do was to build something in memory of our children. There is a school just up the road from our house in Isipingo Hills, in Plett Drive. That is the school our children attended, both Shamima and Humeira. It's a lovely school, the teachers were very good and it was fairly comfortable, just up the road. Sometime after the children passed away, that school was closed and given to the hearing impaired, the deaf children.

Noorjehan had been there several times just to observe and see what was happening. She liked the work that the principal was doing. We had several meetings with the principal and the Board of Trustees of the school. We wanted to know what their requirements were and we were told that they did not have an assessment centre. The only assessment centre for the hearing impaired in Natal was in Pietermaritzburg. From Durban onwards to Port Shepstone there was no assessment centre.

We then decided to donate an assessment centre for the school. We established a very good building with all the latest equipment for assessing hearing impaired children and it was open to everybody, all races. It was named after our daughters; it was named Shahumna Assessment Centre – after Shamima, Humeira and Nadia.

We had a very nice opening ceremony and celebration. They had invited many people to join us and also have dinner. Noorjehan was one of the speakers. She was delighted to have assisted in the creation of the facility. Subsequent to that, the school has been moved to Amanzimtoti in Natal.

Noorjehan continued serving them for some time, until we were approached by the Chatsworth branch of the Hospice. They wanted to establish a fully fledged Hospice in Chatsworth and Noorjehan and I decided that, since they had no funds available at all, we would be the first to contribute.

It took some time because there were negotiations that had to be done, plans to be seen to, and we needed to know what the whole long-term projection was and how they would fund this centre in future. It took up a lot of Noorjehan's time, which was good because she felt she was now contributing of herself. Like Kahil Gibran says, it is good to contribute money, but it is when you contribute of yourself that you truly contribute. This whole process lasted about two years.

It was lovely seeing the building rising from the ground and, subsequently, a year or two after it was built, they obtained a lot more sponsorship from corporates. It has, since, become quite an important centre in Chatsworth. It's one of the bigger and better centres in Natal. Besides the Highway Hospice, it's done very well in terms of maintenance.

We had functions every year. There was Mr Pillay, his wife and his daughter, who were amazing people. They did a lot of wonderful work out there. They regularly have charitable fêtes and dinner dances. The dinner dances brought in quite a bit of money and we assisted them by selling tables and obtaining monetary contributions from other people. It kept Noorjehan quite occupied and also gave her a lot of satisfaction, serving others and seeing the success of the centre.

She began to visit orphanages in Umlazi, Claremont and Lamontville and seeing to their physical needs. At the same time she was very involved in charitable organisations. I think that brought her a lot of joy. She was good at whatever she did and she managed it quite well. Some of her skills had been honed at the time when she helped one of her cousin's friends to deal with her deaf and mute daughter.

Twenty-Three

ADAM: Some three or four years later I tentatively asked Noorjehan if we could have children again, and perhaps start a family once more. She was firmly against the idea. She felt that she was barely coping with her day-to-day life and was in no state to accept further responsibility. Not long after that, we realised that we were getting on in life and it was too late to have children.

We had given serious consideration to the possibility of adopting a child, or perhaps two. Noorjehan was concerned about the genetic consequences and the dangers inherent in selecting someone with a faulty gene pool. We would be taking on a responsibility that would stretch our abilities to the extreme. "Besides," Noorjehan added, "the state of mind I am in I would likely not do justice to my commitment, and that would make me depressed." I realised that as long as that reality existed, adoption was not an option. We agreed that it was best to leave it be.

With the passage of time, our lives took on a semblance of normality. Naturally, there were times when we succumbed to our emotions, especially during the festive periods such as Eid, New Year, the children's birthdays and the anniversary of their death. There were times when we were elated and on the top of a mountain, and there were times when we were plunged into despair and slipped into a valley. Without fail, a few days before each of the above events, the pain would begin to seep into us. We learned to recognize it and found a way to deal with it. That helped us to cope better than drugs or other anti-depressants.

We also learnt to deal with the sadness that enveloped us whenever we attended a wedding. The knowledge that we would never have such an event in our own lives made us gloomy. We found a way to deal with that too. Both Noorjehan and I were making a conscious effort to come to terms with our lives, to accept what we could not change and to pursue vigorously those things that lightened our hearts and lifted our mood.

You could say that we were learning to survive, to establish a degree of stability in our days. We became aware, almost as if for the first time, that any happiness that may come our way **depended entirely on ourselves.** We unconsciously began to acquire a philosophy: we lived for each day at a time, we tackled the major issues immediately and as they arose. We also learned that the foot that goes gets there. Slowly, tentatively, but with determination we began to place one foot in front of the other. As a result, a degree of stability entered our lives.

We were very careful not to kid ourselves into some false sense of security. We accepted that there would be days when we would be plunged into the depths of despair. We found a way to deal with that, to establish a degree of routine and a sense of predictability, some structure and order into our lives. It was a concerted effort, by no means easy, but we soon saw the benefits that flowed from there.

For starters, we decided on a plan that would keep our days full: we began to play badminton regularly, I joined a gym and did some vigorous exercises. And we did a lot of travelling, particularly overseas trips and around-the-world cruises. Quite often, our close friends joined us on these excursions and ensured our enjoyment.

It was not so much the trip itself but rather the planning and the anticipation that heightened our senses and enhanced our mood. And, within this plan of action, we decided that we would live for the day, take one day at a time and not get too involved with aspirations for the future. Five-year plans, as far as we were concerned, were made by countries and not by people.

We hadn't given up entirely on fulfilling our dreams, we were human after all. We simply deferred them, for some future time, but not into too distant a future. Our tragedy had taught us that life is fragile, it could slip through our fingers without giving a moment's notice.

As we tried new activities and new adventures, we began to

learn more about ourselves in many different ways. We saw ourselves through new lenses and from a different perspective. I discovered Noorjehan and she discovered me. We then started understanding each other, and I began to respect her as an individual.

⌘

Initially, when some men marry, we think we have bought a commodity – a slave – and our women become our possessions. Ours is a patriarchal society where we are domesticated and socialised by our parents with a system of reward and punishment. We start wearing masks and become actors and actresses from a tender age, always seeking the reward. Parents socialise us so that we can fit into our society according to its religion and culture, which is necessary for us to integrate and not be left out.

Although we all have personal dreams and desires, our dreams differ according to our cultural norms and the way we were brought up and socialised. Thus, in every relationship, especially the spousal relationship, there are two individual dreams, his dream and her dream, which cannot be merged into one. Because women are heart-orientated and men are head-orientated we experience things differently. We have to respect one another, so we compromise and give each other space. We cannot dictate. But men do tend to dictate – what women wear, eat, drink and, sometimes, even where they may go.

After our tragedy I became more conscious of relationships, more observant and attentive. I realised that each person in a relationship has their own dreams, experiences and baggage that they've accumulated over time. Unfortunately, we are often not really who the other person sees, but rather a projection of what the other wants and expects of us. So we don our masks and create the facades of many different personalities for ourselves; one for our spouse, another for our siblings and parents, and many more for the various others in our lives, such as presidents, colleagues – even beggers in the street. Our attitudes change according to with whom we are relating.

We must guard against trying clear another person's mind of their baggage. Doing so means we do not respect the other and are trying to modify them to make ourselves feel superior and good. Marriage is a team effort where each person participates to the best of their abilities.

Love is an elusive concept and as painful as it is beautiful. Love can be both kind and selfish. Sometimes when we think we are loving another, we're actually striving to possess them. Even the most beautiful cage gilt with diamonds and rubies is constricting. By trying to possess, we ourselves become possessed and imprisoned in the limited constructs of our own mind.

We must strive to respect the uniqueness and dignity of the other. We must not interfere. We must not use another person to meet our own goals and expectations. Real love is unconditional; it fills a much larger space and is less limited.

༜

Now, I realised that I needed to give her as much space as she could have for herself. She had to make her own decisions. Naturally, whenever she wanted my assistance concerning any matter I was there for her. But, ultimately, she lived by her own rules, and, in fairness to her, she was a very considerate and empathetic person. She never abused her new-found liberty, and always conferred with me on any important issue.

Suddenly we became fully-fledged partners in a relationship that was mutually beneficial.

We also learned to accept that resolving conflict in any relationship is a perennial problem. All couples have to deal with such issues; even older people experience discord in their lives. We had reached a stage where we didn't lose our cool or get angry, and we weren't exploding as much as we used to in our initial post-tragedy period. We realised that a relationship should be mutually complementary.

We now freely deferred to each other, and, as a result, a totally new dynamism was introduced into the way we interacted in our day-to-day matters. Our relationship was moving forward in a positive and meaningful way.

And we continued to work at it. We couldn't afford to become complacent and sliding back to our old way of conflict resolution – that would only result in great unhappiness and misery. We were, in a sense, evolving and finding new ways to please each other.

Strangely, our ballroom dancing period put us in touch with scores of people, most of whom had suffered through one form of tragedy or another. The enormity of our own loss made their pain pale into insignificance, and they automatically gravitated towards Noorjehan and phoned her even after we had discontinued our association with the studio.

In a way, Noorjehan became a counsellor and comforted those who had suffered through a bereavement. It was a two-way street, an association that benefited everybody. And none of this positive flow of energy would have been possible **had we given in to society's dictates and just stayed at home, wallowing in our grief.** I often wonder exactly what it was that some people objected to. I can only conclude that their narrow-minded behaviour was a reflection of their own inner unhappiness.

A huge number of these functions were in aid of charity. They were hospice functions, Cancer Association balls, where we not only socialised, but also supported their fund-raising efforts simply by attending their dinners. We also managed to sell a lot of tickets for other charities, such as the blind and deaf societies, so we were quite involved in assisting wherever we could and it was very satisfying and gratifying that we were giving a little of ourselves to society and to the betterment of other people in this world.

I'm not sure how you measure the good that you do in this world, but I think that if anything gives you a warm feeling when you can assist others, then that has to be the ultimate satisfaction. It's not about having too much money, or great fame. I don't think those represent true accomplishments in our life. If somebody asks us what our life was all about, we often respond by saying that we've achieved our goals, we've made a lot of money, we've had our names in the newspapers, we've achieved name and fame. It is good as a marker, but I don't think that is our goal in life. Our accomplishments are what we do in this life, how we treat people, how much happiness we bring to people, how much we empower people. Noorjehan's mantra became, "Where can I assist?"

She also found a great deal of satisfaction in her belief system. She wasn't overtly religious, but she believed that wherever our daughters may be they are in a much better place. And that kept her sane and gave her much comfort.

My belief on the other hand was not strong at all. I was always questioning, and I continue to this day, but I have come to some resolutions in my own mind which have helped me along.

We don't necessarily have to decide on following any fixed principles in our life. I suppose, unlike Noorjehan, because my faith was not that strong, I needed validation. I needed validation of the existence of a God. I needed validation of heaven and hell, that we know is the other side of the coin of life. Strange but true.

The first thing that happens when we are born is we come into this bright light from the beautiful womb, and are smacked on the bottom to awaken us, to bring life into us. But one of the first things our body does is take a breath and that is the sign that life is there, life is around, life has now happened; and the last thing we do when we die, we breathe out. But surely life is more than the simple act of breathing. We are created for some specific purpose, to achieve a set goal. And not knowing exactly what the goal is creates a conflict in our lives, we begin to question the whole purpose of creation. I didn't see that as an aberration. I was provided with a brain, to enable me to think for myself. It was that same brain that was now asking questions and looking for answers.

Through all this, Noorjehan and I were experiencing a form of transformation. Our perception and priorities changed drastically, especially in Noorjehan's case who saw the world through different lenses.

She had attained a sense of serenity that was different from bliss, and would sit quietly for long stretches at a time. She would close her eyes and meditate, which was something that I could unfortunately never do, despite having attended meditation sessions. She had risen above the everyday, feel-good existence that we all have in order to live our lives. We were lonely, yet we got to a stage where we could embrace aloneness.

More than anything in the world, we had each other. We had someone to fall back on when things became too unmanageable. This provided us with a sense of belonging and gave us a feeling of immense security, a harbour to protect us from the rough seas of life. I can truly say that, for the first time, we were beginning to appreciate the meaning of true love.

How was I, a mere mortal, to know that it was a fleeting pleasure, that my serenity would soon implode and I would be cast adrift on the sea of loneliness. Without warning, suddenly and with enormous implications, the diabolic actions of the universe descended upon me. It was a blow that left me reeling and punch-drunk.

Twenty-Four

ADAM: I buried my life, my dreams, my expectations, my lover, my friend, my wife, my teacher, my companion on the 10th of December 2005. With her, I buried my future, my hopes and my dreams. Life today has become my enemy and death my friend.

We had come to a stage in our lives where we felt a little more secure in our own skins. We were more centred in life. We started getting on with the business of living. We built up a very good social circle. Lots of friends and family around us, and life became liveable again, more enjoyable. Sure, we had our ups and downs, we were happy and we were depressed sometimes, but that is what life is all about. We became more enlightened. We did a lot of introspection. We understood life much better than we had ever understood it before. We knew the fragility of life.

I had, by then, semi-retired. I normally left for the surgery around about nine o'clock and came back about three o'clock and had a forty-five minute nap. After that we sat around, possibly going to garden or doing some other things. Normally, at five o'clock every evening, Monday to Friday, we had a routine of sitting in the lounge for two hours listening to music and discussing our day. We needed as much quality time as possible together. This was Noorjehan's idea. On weekends we normally went out for dinner or to some function. It was always during the weekdays that we spent quality time, just the two of us, together.

We were now at the stage where it was okay for just the two of us to go out for supper. In the past we always went out with a group. Now we were quite comfortable in each other's company. We no longer needed a support group to fall back on. We could talk, and we had lots to talk about. We had no need for others to help us open up to each other.

I have noticed that you need to be happy with yourself, to like yourself, before anybody else likes you. Noorjehan and I had both learned this valuable lesson the hard way. It was a lesson that served us very well indeed.

In November of the same year, just before I lost her forever, Noorjehan decided that, for a change, this Christmas she would not like to be in Durban. I suggested that there were friends of ours going to Vietnam and we could join them. She didn't want that. All she wanted was to have a holiday on our own, just the two of us. She was quite adamant that she'd just like us to be alone, with each other. I asked her where she'd like to go, and she suggested Thailand. I made some bookings the following day.

A dear friend of ours, Leslie, had phoned Noorjehan on several occasions and she had sounded very down and quite upset. Her letter, which I set out below, explains her pain.

Dear Noori and Adam

I see you, and would be grateful if you would honour us by making the time to be in our lives. In the three months since our son passed on people have passed by like shadows in twilight. It's as if somehow we know a secret that no one else seems to know, there is no one to share it with, because we live in a land where no one speaks our language, or lives in the same context, so we have unending circular conversations with ourselves. What is or is not important is ephemeral ... momentary, and being this way makes it difficult to connect, but not with the two of you ... and I do not believe that it is generated by a set of similar losses, but in our similar approaches to dealing with those issues.

We have grief, but there is the birth of some other thing, as yet ill defined that neither one of us has yet grasped, but for the first time, seeing the two of you, I have a sense of where we are going, a path you have traveled, and one that we, I, would love to share with you both.

Chris M
Lesley S

Noorjehan then decided to have her over to dinner at our place. We invited her over and she joined us at around seven pm on the ninth of December, and only left after half past twelve. After Leslie had left, Noorjehan complained that she was feeling unaccountably tired and she went off to bed. I then washed the dishes, cleared up, and joined her.

The next morning, a Saturday, Noorjehan remained in bed. I went down, had breakfast and left for the surgery.

Noorjehan phoned me at approximately nine and said that she had run out after me, but I had already left. I told her that I had a patient in the chair and that as soon as I was done I would phone her. I did phone her around ten, but the number was engaged. Normally, on Saturday mornings she would make herself comfortable in the lounge and make her phone calls, to my sisters, to the family and friends. I just assumed that she was speaking to someone.

She had earlier asked our housekeeper, Jabu, to do her Christmas shopping because Jabu has two young girls. She told Jabu, "Do your shopping, come back and then you can retire," because Jabu was leaving for home the following week. I found out about all this much later.

I left the surgery and was looking forward to coming home, for I had finished early, at about eleven thirty. I walked in through the garage door. I was feeling quite cheerful, as we were leaving for our holiday on the following Thursday. I entered the kitchen and shouted for Noorjehan. There was no reply, so I walked into the lounge, expecting to find her there. As I walked in, I saw her lying with the pedestal on the side and she was in the prostrate position, like the Muslims do when they read their prayers.

There was something odd about the way she was lying on the floor, a sort of unnatural pose. Not suspecting anything, I gently tapped her on the shoulder. There was no response. I tapped her again, a little harder. When she didn't move, I became a little agitated and felt for her pulse, and could not find it. That was when I saw the bluish tinge on her fingers. And then it hit me, like a sledgehammer landing on my chest, that I had lost her.

I was still in a stupor when Jabu walked in, took in the scene, and, in a hushed voice asked me what had happened. "I think Noorjehan is gone," I replied, hardly believing my own words.

Looking at Noorjehan lying there on the floor, my body and mind were totally numb. I was a robot but, inside me, I was screaming like a mad man. I was not sure what to do. I was dazed, confused and in a state of shock. Jabu let out a scream that pierced through the house and she became uncontrollable, sobbing.

I was moving like an automaton. From somewhere I collected a blanket and covered my dear wife. I was still in a daze when I phoned the paramedics and my close friends and family, both in Durban and Balfour. I didn't need the paramedics to tell me that I had lost Noorjehan. I was a medical doctor myself, I **knew** she was gone. I was frozen to the spot, my brain refusing to register the reality before me. And then I began to tremble, my body started to shake violently. I realised then that I was actually sobbing.

Within minutes, my friends had arranged for a hearse to come over. I followed the hearse to a hall up the road where the women bathed Noorjehan and prepared her for burial. To this day I thank the universe for giving me good and true friends. Saantha Naidu and Ayesha Mahomed wrapped their arms around me. From that moment on they remained close to me, and helped me to retain my sanity.

From somewhere deep inside me I found the strength to make some crucial decisions – one of which was that I would take Noorjehan to Balfour and bury her next to our daughters.

It took us forever getting to Balfour. On reaching Balfour, we carried the coffin out of the hearse and we laid her out on the floor, according to Muslim custom. The whole room had been cleared, and she was wrapped in calico and put on the floor on the blankets. All the women were sitting and praying there. Even in my stunned state of mind, I couldn't help noticing that she was in the very spot where our daughters had been laid out.

Within an hour and a half after we got to Balfour, we went to the graveyard and lowered the body into the grave. Noorjehan's brother and his son joined me, and the three of us ensured that the body was in the correct position before being covered with some planks to protect the coffin from direct contact with the sand.

By that evening I was totally and completely fatigued. To make matters worse, I had gone through a huge number of cigarettes on the trip from Durban and my throat was feeling quite foul.

After the funeral, it's a custom in our community to feed people who had travelled long distances. As a result it was about ten, ten thirty before I could go to bed. I had taken some sleeping tablets. They didn't help much and I tossed and turned through a sleepless night.

The next day there was a flow of people that came over to sympathise. On that Monday, I headed back to Durban, to my home. Once there, I found it easier to deal with my grief, in the privacy of my room. I no longer had to deal with people, however well-meaning they may have been.

There was a strange acceptance in my mind that wherever the children had gone, she would meet them sometime. My belief was purely an emotional reaction rather than a process of reason, unlike Noorjehan who always believed in that concept fully. However, her biggest fear was losing me before she herself passed on. Because of our age difference, I am twelve years older than her, and because men tend to die earlier, she was projecting another twenty years that she would have to live after I was gone. And she'd wish for two things; she'd always wish for an early, peaceful death, where she would not have become a dependant, and the other was that she would go before me.

I was totally numb. It's the brain's way of self-preservation of our mental state, so that we can come to grips with our huge loss. Numbness is like a shock absorber, it allows our brain to absorb the doomsday scenario. None of this helped me much. I was at a sort of life's dead end – a zombie.

I suppose preparing for the funeral and attending to the necessary arrangements kept my mind occupied, a form of distraction during this period of chaos and helplessness.

Seeing her lying on the floor in Balfour, just before the funeral, I knew that she'd taken away a very large chunk of me. She had taken away all my hopes and my dreams. And yet I knew, deep down, that if there is another life and she had gone from the physical to the spiritual, and if she could look down, she would be happy. I was also angry, she was too young to die, but who is to determine what is the right time to die? I'm always reminded that death follows no definite timetable, but chooses its own time and place.

At funerals we are forced to keep on relating the events leading to death to everybody. How it happened, where was I when it happened, what was the cause and so on and on. I suppose there's comfort and relief that comes through the expression of feelings, the release of pent-up tears and the uncovering of sorrow as we talk to those who want to listen. We tend to unburden ourselves and we feel much lighter by sharing our grief. Unfortunately, during my daughters' deaths I could not express my feelings and got stuck emotionally. It took me much longer to come out of my depression.

The repetition of the story allowed me to dissipate and share the pain. I also remembered more of Noorjehan's life and other people gave me feedback on her which was very reassuring and satisfying. I wanted her life to matter.

My family insisted that I stay in Balfour for some time. However, I was very restless and asked my brother to take me through to Johannesburg International Airport, to get a flight back to Durban. When I came home Jabu was crying and sobbing. We sat together, talking about Noorjehan, after which I spent a lot of time alone in my bed. I needed to cry and with Jabu around, I was quite comfortable, as she was sobbing too. We were both inconsolable.

For the first week I was constantly answering the phone and responding to the door bell. Gradually, the flow of visitors decreased and the phone calls petered out. And then the loneliness hit me. I could no longer hide behind the phone calls and all the visitors. The world goes on and you feel like a stranger, in no mood to talk about material or political matters. I couldn't believe that the world went on so normally, as if nothing had happened, whilst my own world had collapsed.

After another week I decided to throw myself back into my work, but it was very difficult. I tried. I took in one patient and half way through I couldn't contain my emotions. I was battling to get a rhythm and a pattern back in my life. I tried to live on a day to day basis. Going to the surgery, taking a walk around Pinetown and just strolling aimlessly. I'd take a slow walk and observe the whole world passing by. It was therapeutic. The hardest part of the day was going back home, to an empty nest.

Twenty-Five

ADAM: I think the most acute pain comes a few days after death. At the time of death, because of the funeral and because of your denial and shock, it doesn't fully hit you. But, a few days after death, there's the numbing shock of your great loss. The stunned feelings come alive sharply. I was too overwhelmed by a deep longing to see Noorjehan. The grief was all absorbing. There was sadness, there was emotional pain, bouts of harsh sobbing and, surprisingly, also anger. And, within it all, I felt immensely tired. I was continuously tired. Although I took sleeping tablets, I slept fitfully, but getting up in the morning, I felt this aching and tiredness. I wanted to sleep forever, with the curtains closed and not see any daylight. It was a form of hibernation, hoping for better and sunny days.

The knowledge that this is how my life would be, that I would be all on my own for the rest of my days, was unbearable agony. And then I retreated into myself, creating a space to vent my anger and frustration. And when that failed to relieve my grief, I looked for some other outlet. I considered the possibility of some form of physical diversion.

I took up golf, even going for private lessons and spending a big part of my day on the practice range. Nothing helped! The hollow feeling in my wounded heart refused to go away.

The hardest part of my day was during the evening. This was the time when Noorjehan would sit beside me and we would chat about how our respective day had been, or plan a dinner or a trip to somewhere. Now I found myself all alone on the patio, smoking a few cigarettes, trying to make sense of what life was all about. Eventually, with a heavy sigh I would seek sanctuary in my bed, only to find that it was as empty as the rest of me.

I would then jump out of bed, walk around aimlessly and, in the dressing room, look at Noorjehan's clothing and smell the faint hint of her being. That was when the pain became unbearable. Once more, I would head for the patio. I would just stand there, in my mind I could hear the music that had always been playing in the background. For a fleeting moment I never failed to sense her presence, a strong feeling of déjà vu, a leap into the recent past.

It was a very brief diversion. Back in my bedroom, I'd turn on the TV and try to follow the news. But I found it impossible to concentrate on the picture and simply switched it off again.

In the midst of all this upheaval, I knew, deep inside me, that I would have to find a way of dealing with life, to accept the reality of my lonely existence and come to grips with myself. It was a task of immense proportions, and the comments of well-meaning and well-intentioned people made matters worse. They acted automatically, perhaps believing that saying something inappropriate was preferable to saying nothing at all.

It became increasingly difficult for me to appear in public. It happened, at times, that people tried to avoid me, simply because they didn't know what to say or how to interact with me. But I couldn't, obviously, make a complete break with society. I couldn't live in isolation forever.

I made a concerted effort to appear quite normal and at peace with myself. I answered the usual questions with a degree of equanimity. I responded to the displays of sympathy in a contained and stoic manner. I had to draw on all my reserves of strength simply to nod gratefully.

I was aware that I had to find a way to handle each day, one day at a time. I had sufficient respect in my ability to keep my grief to myself. But first, I had to hive off into a corner, assess my situation, allow my thoughts to flow freely without fighting the emotions they invoked.

Slowly, reluctantly, my mind went into freefall. I allowed my emotions to wash over me, not resisting the impulse to deny the pain. I was, in a way, saying to myself, "Okay, let it all come out, face up to it and then find a way to move on."

What kind of future did I have? I was no longer a husband, or a father. I was in a house, but it did not feel like a home. Those were the first things that I had to deal with. I couldn't deny that there was this total void in my life, that was suddenly empty and devoid of life, companionship and family. I was also aware that life, as one usually knows it, was not about money, power, name and fame.

I tried to use the distraction technique. I tried to read. Reading the morning newspaper was a chore, I found it hard to concentrate. Eating breakfast was a tasteless, but necessary, requirement. My mind was like a beehive, buzzing incessantly but not producing honey, just full of dark, dreary thoughts.

I feel sad at the loss of a potential future and my own connection to it. I grieve for the loss of my role as a husband. It's a total void in my life which makes me feel unhappy and completely useless and empty. Our happiness arises from love, companionship, friends and family. It's not about money, power, name and fame and yet I lost the very anchor that had grounded me to the earth plane.

Life, I concluded, was about companionship, of getting into the car, of sitting in the evenings just talking, of going to the supermarket, of laughing, sharing a joke, of watching TV, holding hands, just going for a walk or hugging a loved one, knowing the existence and the presence of the other. This was what we had invested our future in, a future that was now bankrupted by the loss of all my dreams.

Grieving, on the other hand, is like moving into a long, dark tunnel, or, rather, falling into a long, dark tunnel, an unwilling participant or walking into it, pushed into it against your will. Once you are in the tunnel you lose all sense of time and direction. There is no way out. You have to move on because the door is shut, and as you move along, you're hoping with hope that there will be light at the end of the tunnel. There will be an acceptance of death. There'll be some sort of realisation that life will come back to some form of normality.

As you grope inside the tunnel, there are intense feelings of loneliness, the grieving stage of a cocktail of emotions in your life.

You cannot see any future. It's all doom and gloom. You often wonder whether there will be a future, because the desire is to go back in time and retrieve the past, this is the most intense period of grieving.

You cannot do more than try to react to the dark. What will happen? Will you ever experience happiness again? Will there be laughter in your life, or will life be one bleak, tortuous future?

You cannot imagine it now but maybe some time, hopefully life will be kind.

The period in the middle of the tunnel is in fact the most depressing one. You become totally numb, and you're not aware, at this time, that it's a self-preservation thing. It gives the mind the time to heal and allow small doses of acceptance and acknowledgement. Yes, maybe depression seeps in because it is a self-preservation thing.

And, as these thoughts consumed me, I felt depressed, to the point of no return.

And then there was the guilt. I felt very guilty when I went off that Saturday morning. I set off very early because there was a meeting at seven-thirty. I normally go at nine o'clock. I felt guilty leaving home and not hearing Noorjehan call after me.

I went to the surgery and, when she phoned me, I said, "I'll return your call as soon as I've finished with my patient." Immediately after finishing with the patient, I did phone, but I assumed she was engaged for two reasons: because it was a new phone and she didn't know how to use it or, alternatively, she may have been busy with my sisters who she normally phoned on a Saturday morning. So I simply said to myself, "She's most probably busy."

Not suspecting anything untoward, I left the surgery about eleven o'clock. She had asked me to run an errand for her, to call on the lady who makes pickles. She had already placed an order and had asked me to collect the items, because she needed to distribute this to the Transvaal. I attended to that.

All these memories were circling around within me, with the events of the last few weeks playing on my mind. There was a dinner that we had, a function we had attended. It worried me that during it all there had been no forewarning, a hint of what lay ahead.

Experiencing all this guilt, I quietly withdrew from society. What people saw of me was a fraction. My inner and outer worlds were totally different. My inner was in a total state of upheaval, while the outer was in control.

I only became aware much later that talking actually does help, though the majority do not fully comprehend what I was saying. However, there were some that did understand my pain. This did not make it easier. It hurts sometimes when you talk with someone else, about your deepest experiences and emotions, and you suspect that what you are saying is not fully appreciated by the other person.

That was when I began questioning the meaning of life, and thoughts of suicide were not uncommon. However, it is the acceptance of what has happened in the past, which is the most difficult thing for any human being to handle, and yet we know and understand that all seasons in life, the good, bad, happy, sad, all come and go in their own time.

Somewhere, within these thoughts, I realised that it was necessary to expand my network of friends. My whole world and life had changed, as a single man I had to check out my strengths and weaknesses, which would cater for my physical and emotional needs. There are no quick fixes or replacements in order to lead a worthwhile life.

After Noorjehan's death, people were urging me to sell the house and move to new premises, starting afresh. I'm glad I resisted the advice, as this house has many sentimental and beautiful memories. There is a comfort in knowing that this was Noorjehan's castle, and she put her heart and soul and lots of effort into building and decorating this house.

You carry your memories like a shadow, which follows you wherever you are. It was easier for me, in familiar surroundings, to retrieve and relive the memories of my beloved near and dear ones. Why leave the memories behind, when there is a familiarity in your mind's eye and you can picture your partner in her own space.

The most difficult times were the weekends and holidays. That was when we used to visit our friends. My good friends still ask me to travel abroad, to get away for a while, but it would not be the same as there would be no shared experiences. Now the pleasures and beauties I take in would be mine alone and not ours. With Noorjehan, it was sharing experiences at different levels, as husband and wife; her friends, my friends, common friends.

Is there such a thing as closure? Grief is a process to live through. It is linear, and as time goes by there are longer and longer periods of serenity. It is not like a circle where there is a beginning and an end. At times you are happy and normal and suddenly sadness descends like a bolt of lightning without any warning.

However it is a gradual process although the scars remain forever. You never get over it but you learn to live with it. You do not fall apart as you did during the early stages. You heal, but your world and priorities change. I now have to rearrange my daily activities around me alone. New meaning, new beginning, but you can't forget the past. You carry the pain of grief within where also resides the process of healing. I know now that companionship, once lost, can never be recovered. I am now entering a new world, without wearing too many masks.

We move forward and cannot find the exact time, the day and the month that signifies the healing is complete and that tells us that we're done with grief.

Sometimes I think the tragedy, drawbacks and friction in our lives are like the initiation in tribes, that mark the passage from childhood to adulthood. If we persevere and believe in ourselves then we become stable by accessing our inner resources, which we do not know that all of us inherently possess. Because we have faced death, we are now ready to tackle life in a more productive, proactive, mature and kind outlook, and in a new state of consciousness.

After the tragedy, over a long period of introspection, it is possible to live life more richly, with maturity and understanding that death is a part of life and that it eventually overtakes us all.

Support groups are generally very helpful where we develop meaningful relationships. A whole new routine in your lives together.

And yes, life does go on. Who knows what tomorrow will bring. Will the sun shine? Will there be rain? Or will it just be overcast? Will some great power – what some refer to as the **universe** – wave a magic wand and, suddenly, eliminate all our pain?

I can only stand and wait – an observer as my life unfolds. But that suggests that I am a spectator, watching a game in process, unable to influence the end result in any way. I cannot accept this. I will not, I cannot, I refuse to accept that the loss of my entire family, the destruction of my dreams, is simply a process of random events. To believe that would be a denial of the purpose behind the creation of humanity.

If there is no purpose governing our existence on this earth then the entire **miracle** of birth, of the **creation of life**, becomes senseless. And I cannot subscribe to such nonsensical beliefs.

A miracle, of the magnitude of birth, the beauty of the human body, the marvel that are our eyes, the wonder of our heartbeat and the phenomenon that is our senses, **does not simply happen!** Some power out there has to be co-ordinating it, and that it all has to be part of some masterplan which at the moment evades me. Ah! Sweet mystery of life!

I live in the hope that, whatever that plan is, it will be revealed to me. And, together with it, the knowledge of the whereabouts of my loved ones. That has to happen, as night follows day – a natural progression.

It is my birthright.
It is why I was created.
It is why I was blessed with a brain.
And it is what gives me hope to go on.

Epilogue

Over the ages, wise men have always said that life is unpredictable - in the midst of life we are in death.

Some wit once reasoned that life is a bee – on some days it gives you honey, on others it stings you.

I have tasted of the honey, and winced when I was stung. Through it all, I've learnt that each day is a gamble and the odds are stacked against you.

It is not about winning or losing, but about how you play the game.

Shakespeare put it very succinctly, when he wrote:

All the world's a stage
And all the men and women merely players.
They have their exits and their entrances;
And one man in his time plays many parts.

I would like to think that I played my part honourably and gracefully.

It is all that I have to offer to the memory of my dear departed loved ones. The storm that swept over me has passed.

I must move on, wherever that road may lead me. And I rest secure in the knowledge that we will be together again, that all paths eventually lead to a reunion.

I have to believe in that, implicitly. It is the shield that protects my sanity. And keeps me on an even keel.

And now, in the November of my life, it is the dream that restores my reason and gives me the strength to venture into that long dark night.

Can December be all that far away?

To the Shahumna Assessment Centre

Some of the people must be wondering why Adam is not at the podium – simple – I am the boss. The new constitution allows this type of affirmative action.

Thank you for that kind introduction, it seems that now I shall have to say two prayers for forgiveness. The first for my introducer for flattering me so much, the second for myself for enjoying it so much. The Principal, Mrs Naidoo, the Board of Management and Staff of the Durban School for the Hearing Impaired, Honoured Guests, Ladies and Gentlemen.

At the very outset we must thank you for attending and sharing with us the official opening of the Shahumna Assessment Centre. For those who don't know Adam and I, we are the parents of our three beloved daughters, Shamima, Humeira and Nadia whom we lost in a car accident on the second of March 1986.

What happened to us is what one reads in the papers and is something beyond one's wildest imagination. It seems too farfetched for anyone to lose their entire family within an hour, but it happened. Our lives had suddenly and unexpectedly taken a course that appears both uncharted and endless. Bewildered we vainly searched for pathways back to our former lives until we confronted the reality. There was no way back. Our options were limited. Either we go into a form of hopeless vegetation or we re-invest in our lives. Although we found nothing the same again.

You parents have hope. Our hopes and dreams and envisions have all gone with our children. No-one chooses the events that happen in life. No-one chooses to be born at certain times. No-one chooses to be handicapped or bereaved parents. We have experienced many unfamiliar feelings during the early part of our grief and realise that crying, being angry and expressing our feelings was better than suppressing our feelings. We also experienced feelings of intense pain, isolation, exhaustion, panic,

144

fear, deep depression, anger and guilt. Grief is extremely painful but it is the cost of commitment to those we love. We have been seeking for some time an institution to perpetuate the memory of our beloved daughters. We have visited many handicapped institutions where we have found many dedicated people doing some excellent work.

However, the track record of the Principal, Mrs Naidoo, and her dedicated and loyal staff have been outstanding. Incidentally, our daughters Shamima and Humeira had attended the then Isipingo Primary School at these premises. We are proud to be associated with the Durban School for the Hearing Impaired.

In dealing with handicapped pupils, one has to become totally and wholly involved and get immersed into their daily lives. Obviously, with this type of relationship you share equally in their emotions. There can be joy and there can be heartache and sacrifices.

I must strongly emphasise that I like the holistic and hands-on approach that Mrs Naidoo and her team have adopted. By holistic I mean treating the whole child. The communication skills, the social skills, the emotional well-being, their health and welfare.

They have gone one step further by extending the concept in encompassing the parents as well.

I would like to compliment Mrs Naidoo and her management team, Mr Arvind Kisoon Singh and Gora Akoob and Ahmed Jooma for their total dedication and management of this institution in these difficult and trying times where there is a constant battle for funds from the education department and from businesses, who I must confess, are going through trying times.

I know the personal commitment and perseverance and sacrifices that public and civic work entails.

Let us pray that the Almighty bless and assist the forces that make this wonderful institution tick to climb to even greater heights.

I am certain that the Shahumna Assessment Centre will be a great help, not only to this school but through the whole of the

South Coast referral base.

We would like to congratulate all the pupils and wish them every success in their exams.

To the parents of these children, I would like to share something I have learnt, that God will not let you carry a cross heavier than you can bear. Learn to flow with your feelings and know that although they are initially painful they are not permanent. With grit, determination and prayer, we all tend to function again. With every obstacle that God places in our path, we tend to grow and become more compassionate.

Once again, on behalf of my husband, Adam, and myself, I would like to thank Mrs Naidoo for having given us this opportunity to address you.

Before I conclude, Khalil Gibran speaks to us of giving:

"You give but little when you give of your possessions. It is when you give of yourself that you truly give. There are those who give little of the much that they have and they give it for recognition and their hidden desire makes their gifts unwholesome. There are those who have little and give it all. These are the believers in life and the bounty of life and their coffer is never empty. There are those who give with joy and that joy is their reward and there are those who give with pain and that pain is their baptism. It is well to give when asked but it is better to give unasked through understanding, therefore give now, that is the season of giving, maybe yours and not your inheritors."

Thank you.

• Transcript of a speech made by Noojehan on the occasion of the opening of the Shahumna Assessment Centre, December 1996

To the Rotary Club

Chairman, Rotarians, Annes of Isipingo Rotary Club and guests. Good evening.

I wish to take this opportunity in thanking you for the invitation you have extended to us.

For those who don't know Adam and myself, we are the parents of our beloved daughters Shamima, Humeira and Nadia whom we lost in a car crash on the second of March 1986.

What happened to us is something that one reads in the papers or one watches in the movies. It seemed too far fetched to happen to anyone. To lose all our children within the space of one hour – but it happened and in minutes our lives were totally shattered into tiny bits and so very difficult to put together.

The initial stages are of shock and the feeling of absolute numbness. Suddenly, everything has changed and now comes the 'ifs' and 'whys'? If we didn't go that weekend this would not have happened. Why, why, why, why us? What have we done to deserve this? There are no answers to that and I realise there never will be.

We experienced many unfamiliar feelings during the first year of grief and we realise that crying, being angry, expressing our feelings was better than bottling it all up. We also experienced intense pain, feelings of unreality, isolation, exhaustion, panic fear, deep depression, anger and guilt. We thought we were going crazy. Grief is extremely painful but it is the cost of commitment to those we love. Grief is a process and as such has a beginning and never truly an end. It is hard work but the only way to reach the other side is to go through it.

Learn to flow with your feelings and know that although they are painful, they are not permanent. Your sense of reality, your concentration, will come back and you will function again although your pain and memories will be your constant companions.

And in our case, having lost all our children, there wasn't only the loss to deal with but our marriage was at stake as well. Adam and I, being so close for thirteen years, took minutes to drift poles apart. Fortunately, both of us worked hard towards our marriage and we are even closer now. We now realise that children are the bonding element in a marriage.

When tragedy strikes, we expect to be able to lean on our husband or wife. It is a shock to find that it is hard to lean on somene who is already double bent. Learn to accept and respect each other's methods of grieving even if you don't understand.

I had no reason to question anything at one time. Like most people I have total faith in God and suddenly realise that religion is blind faith and I wanted to know is there a hereafter? Where are my children? Are they missing us as much as we are missing them?

And I started searching for some sort of peace of mind and to know my babies are somewhere in the land of God and well taken care of. It was a testing time for our religious beliefs.

Reading helped us a great deal. Adam and I were both very angry with God for doing this to us and very bitter towards the world (more Adam than me). The months went by during the first year. There is a first time for everything. Like I went to the supermarket and it struck me that the last time I was here the children were with me and on and on it went for the whole year. Now it is nearly four years since we last saw our babies. Four years have gone by very quickly and painfully but the physical missing seems like forty years.

The missing is so severe at times and the feeling of helplessness and it is at this time that one turns to God where that few minutes of meditating and having a talk with God helps. One realises that death is so final, whatever religion one belongs to. I believe we pray to that one God in many different ways and manners.

During our period of grief, we found that many people did not know how to approach us with the result that they shied away from us. To the person who has lost loved ones your visit and presence means a lot to them and if you don't know what to tell that person, you can say what you mean, "I really don't know what to tell you," or, "I feel for you very much".

You will hear all kinds of comments, "Hold your chin up", "Well you can have more children", "I know just how you feel because I lost my ninty-six year old grandmother last year." Sometimes it will hurt, sometimes make you angry, most people mean well, they are not out to hurt you, they just don't know what to say. It is a wonderful feeling to know that people care and these are the times when they are most appreciated.

I've commonly found people saying, "I don't want to remind you of the past," believe me nobody can remind you. Speaking for myself, I sleep with it, I get up with it and I walk with it. I also want to talk about the children, even if it means I break down. I find crying an excellent therapy, let the tears roll down 'til there are not tears anymore. I can now fully understand the phrase, "Behind every smile there is a tear."

As Khalil Gibran says:

"Your children are not your children. They are the sons and daughters of life's longing for itself. They come through you but not from you and although they are with you, they belong not to you. You may give them your love but not your thoughts for they have their own thoughts. You may house their bodies but not their souls. For their souls dwell in the house of tomorrow, which you cannot visit, not even in your dreams. You may strive to be like them but seek not to make them like you. For life goes not backwards, nor tarries with yesterday."

Thank you for sharing this with us as death is a topic not everyone wants to hear but I must tell you of one good thing that came from this tragedy is that I don't fear death like I used to. Death has become our friend, we look forward to the day when we shall be reunited with our loved ones.

Thank you once again, and also a very special thank you to my dear husband Adam, Shivaz and our close friends, Vasie and Hoosen.

For those of you who have been there through our trying times, thank you. And also to those who have been judgmental towards us, we also say thank you very gracefully as well but also sometimes, as "society" people we all have a lot to learn in life as well as life is a learning lesson.

With love and thoughts to all who have lost loved ones and also to the people who are ill. Let there be a good support system and project good energies and thoughts.

God Bless.

• An address by Noorjehan at the Rotary Club in 1988, one of many that she made.

At the launch of this book

Thank you to all who accepted our invitation to the launch of this book. And thanks to all who live elsewhere and could not attend but have picked this book up for examination.

Although this has been a very emotional evening, I am glad that the book has seen the light of day.

In the beginning, Noorjehan put pen to paper as a form of catharsis. It was very painful reliving the tragedy and releasing the buried thoughts from her unconscious to her conscious mind. The idea at the time was to release some of the pent up emotions – it was never about publishing. Hers was a private and personal journey.

She was a constant visitor to Professor Fatima Meer, who suggested that it would be therapeutic for Noorjehan to write about her experiences in fighting the demons of her tragedy. So, Noorjehan showed Fatima her manuscript and was encouraged to pursue the passion and articulate her sentiments, feelings and challenges in written form. I was asked to give my version.

This book was written to bring support and strength to other bereaved people. Tragedy creates loneliness, guilt, anger, frustration, fear and yearning, which can overtake our very existence. This book is to share and help others learn how to cross this tsunami with a little more confidence and understanding. Those who have lost someone know that it is the most painful and debilitating experience one will ever encounter. Yet, society underestimates the depth of this distress and expects people to just "get over it". The distressed need a fellow traveller who will empathise with understanding and compassion.

Pain is the greatest motivator for change. Helping others facilitates healing and make helps you make sense of the senseless. If we do not have love in our lives then we escape grief, for grief is the price we pay for love, which makes living worthwhile. Whether we lose a spouse, a child, a parent, a brother or a sister, pain awaits us and when it comes we have to confront and experience it before it can be eased.

Grief is not confined to bereavement; it can be the result of losing a limb, of divorce, a toxic marriage, addictions, physical and/or psychological abuse. Where there is suffering there is emotional pain.

In the early days we were hopelessly searching, desperately searching, constantly searching for our daughters. Were they in a better place? Were they happy? Were they missing us as much as we were missing them?

Normally we accept the existence of God but in a tragedy we question his existence. Is there a merciful, compassionate and loving creator?

If so, what was the tragedy about? And WHY US?

I was angry with God. My faith was shattered. I stopped believing and professed to become an atheist. Noorjehan always thought that I was a sceptic because I needed validation and proof of the existence of God. I needed something tangible. She often asked if love and happiness were tangible. These are not things we can grasp in our hands.

Noorjehan had more serenity than I. She grasped onto faith, which allowed her to shift responsibility to the creator and share her load with a greater power, attributing the tragedy to destiny or *Taqdir*. The Chinese, during traumatic times, would often say that "the stars were not in a straight line", thus shifting and sharing responsibility. This lightens the burden. In Chinese there is no such word as "crisis". Depicted by drawn characters, the illustration has two meanings: crisis or opportunity.

We know that all crises can be teachers and it is how we relate to our problems that makes the difference.

Noorjehan was fortunate to have had visions of our daughters, which gave her peace of mind. Whenever she awoke with a severe headache in the morning I knew that she had been with our daughters and was having what she called a "happy headache". We often discussed whether this was just a dream or astral travel.

Was it an out-of-body experience or does our consciousness travel while we are asleep?

Science maintains two dimensions: the known and the unknown ... soon the unknown will be the known. Mystics talk about the third dimension, the unknowable. Who is to pass judgement on the veracity of the above statements?

Noorjehan had her own philosophies about the problems in our lives.

She maintained that there were God-given problems and man-made problems. The God-given we can do nothing about, the man-made we can.

As she surrendered to the will of the universe, I realised that, with tragedy, we'd grown to understand some of life's truisms. Most of life is about surrendering something over which we have no control. Some days we are happy and some days we are sad. When happy, enjoy the moment, sing and dance and do not hold on to it. On the days when you are sad, then be sad, sing sad songs and allow the sadness to be part of your life.

We have no control. When sadness comes, accept it. It has something to give that no happiness can give you. Happiness is shallow, like the wave of the ocean. Sadness is like the deeper part of the sea.

Consider the saying, "when you laugh the world laughs with you, when you cry, you cry alone". In happiness you move with the crowd. In sadness you remain with yourself ... all alone. You have to find your inner resources. You have to look within your inner temple – your inner shrine and into your mind.

When God created the universe, he resided on earth. His advisers suggested they live on Mount Kilimanjaro. God mentioned that someone like Edmund Hillary would climb the mountain. When other advisors suggested that they live on the moon, God retorted by saying, "I am God, so I know that man will one day travel to the moon". A quiet, meditative advisor suggested that God live within man, where man never looks, as he rarely does introspection.

The great Prophet Mohamed, Jesus, Moses, Buddha and Krishna all found their God within, through meditation. They were like rivers; individuals who finally merged to become one with the sea, losing their individuality in the process. I strongly believe that by introspection we can achieve an inner sanity and meditative quality.

Once you accept sadness it is no longer sadness, as you have brought a new quality to it. You have now integrated both happiness and sadness into your soul, thus decreasing anxiety and stress in your daily life. This is the duality of life. Although we always prefer the happier side of the coin, toss it and sorrow follows.

I am often asked if there is contentment after a tragedy and my answer has been, is there contentment in life? Farid was a great Sufi, whose villagers requested that he visit the Mogul Emperor as they desperately needed a school in the village. Farid went to Delhi and was escorted to the Emperor's Mosque where he stood behind Akbar, who was saying his prayer. As he ended, all raised their hands towards the sky in supplication and heard Akbar asking God for more territory. On hearing this, Farid stood up and walked out. Akbar's disciple ran after Farid and asked him his reason for walking out. Farid replied that he had come to request a school in the village but after hearing the prayer realised that the Emperor was too poor to accede to his request. The moral of the story is that most of our lives we sleep walk. So we must develop awareness and consciousness. What this great Emperor was doing is what humanity does every day. Desires live in the future and by their very nature are unquenchable.

- We should not be possessed by our wealth, work or fame.
- We should be possessors.
- We should control our wealth, work and life and not be possessed.
- We cannot postpone our life as our inbox will never be empty.
- We will not only put our life on hold but miss out on our spouse and children.
- A great price to pay.

We have in our lives a good family, spouse and friends.

We have to evolve and not stagnate; we must practice spousal compromise, partnership, respect, reverence – worship and being happy within one's self.

Is there closure? Life is a journey and not a destination.

In the Middle East they have a custom were they tear the *abaya* and sow it together, showing that one is whole after fragmenting into pieces.

I am ready to wear my grief on my sleeve and not put on too many masks. My grief needs to be witnessed by all.

There is a gradual acceptance. We make changes in our lives, adapt to our altered circumstances and thereby face the reality of our loss.

This is learning to live without your anchor.

There is always light at the end of the tunnel, depending on your mind set.

To Noorjehan, this is a celebration of your life and a legacy we leave behind. I salute you and thank you for it.

And to people everywhere, you are all winners. And whatever your dreams, dream on and make it a mission to serve your people and leave a legacy. For we live but once. Life is not a dress rehearsal. Do enjoy this moment, for the future is a desire of our projections and not a reality.

Adam Mahomed
3 December 2010

Looking into Darkness

For six months I lived under a self-imposed news blackout — I did not read the newspapers or watch television. The reason was that I could not withstand the way my person was being portrayed by our local media. It was painful to see one's life being twisted into that of a monster.

Then this morning something unique happened, which elucidated an upsurge of hope; something turned toward the future. I had somehow misplaced my wristwatch and need to find out the time. As I was flipping through the channels, whether by fate or pure coincidence, I tuned in to SABC TV 2, where Dr Adam Mahomed was being interviewed by Leanne Manas. When asked "How does it feel to lose your children and later your wife," Dr Mahomed answered, "There was nothing to live for, and my life lost its meaning and bearing". "And how did you cope?" With tears in his eyes Dr Mahomed emotionally replied, "I at least have my faith and that is all that I had then".

It was this episode this morning that inspired me to make a special request to speak this evening, which is quite out of character. Dr Mahomed, your story, as beautifully and elegantly presented in this book, is all about life with its uncertainties. I am inspired by your courage and your faith, by the deep love you still feel for your departed family and by the way you have transformed your pain into so many good works of charity.

I would like to leave you with a poem, which is one of my favourites — and one that inspired my father-in-law, Nelson Mandela, not to give up during his long years in prison.

• Speech by Dr Kwame Amuah at the Johannesburg launch of this book. March 30th, 2011, The Inanda Club

Invictus

Out of the night that covers me,
Black as the Pit from pole to pole,
I thank whatever gods may be
For my unconquerable soul.

In the fell clutch of circumstance
I have not winced nor cried aloud.
Under the bludgeonings of chance
My head is bloody, but unbowed.

Beyond this place of wrath and tears
Looms but the Horror of the shade,
And yet the menace of the years
Finds, and shall find, me unafraid.

It matters not how strait the gate,
How charged with punishments the scroll.
I am the master of my fate:
I am the captain of my soul.

William Ernest Henley